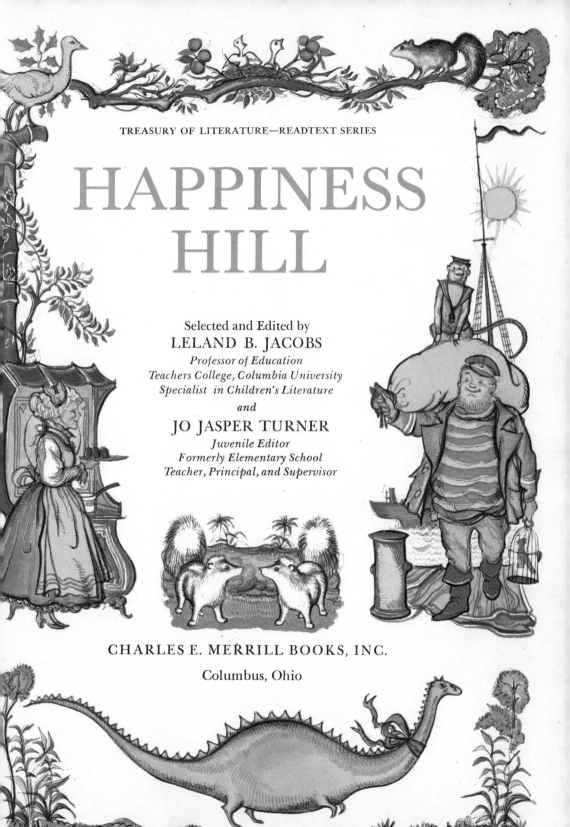

TREASURY OF LITERATURE—READTEXT SERIES

HAPPINESS HILL

Selected and Edited by
LELAND B. JACOBS
Professor of Education
Teachers College, Columbia University
Specialist in Children's Literature
and
JO JASPER TURNER
Juvenile Editor
Formerly Elementary School
Teacher, Principal, and Supervisor

CHARLES E. MERRILL BOOKS, INC.

Columbus, Ohio

TREASURY OF
Readtext Series
LITERATURE

The books in this series are:

MERRY-GO-ROUND
•

HAPPINESS HILL
• •

TREAT SHOP
• • •

MAGIC CARPET
• • • •

ENCHANTED ISLES
• • • • •

ADVENTURE LANDS
• • • • • •

CHARLES E. MERRILL BOOKS, INC.
1300 ALUM CREEK DRIVE • COLUMBUS 16, OHIO

© Copyright, 1960, by Charles E. Merrill Books, Inc. and Artists and Writers Press, Inc.
Printed in the U.S.A. by Western Printing and Lithographing Company. Published
simultaneously in Canada by Thomas Nelson & Sons (Canada) Limited.

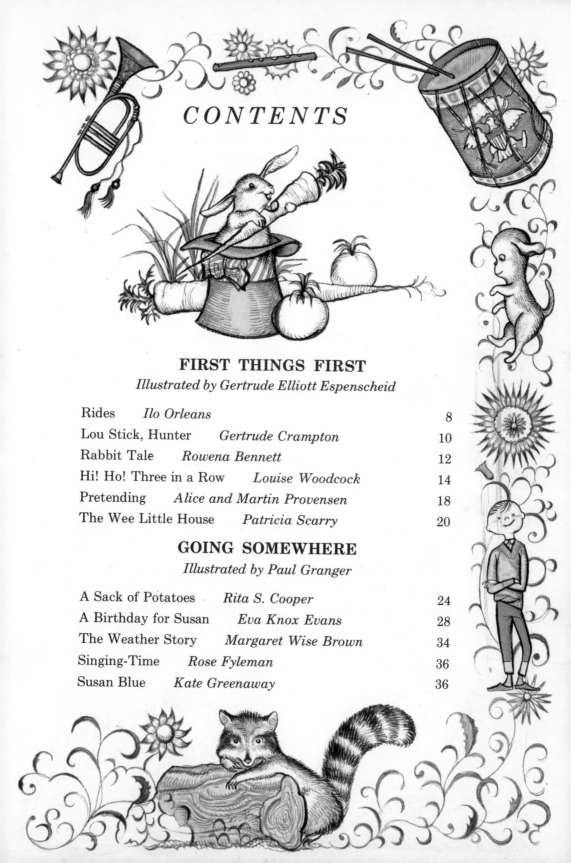

CONTENTS

FIRST THINGS FIRST

Illustrated by Gertrude Elliott Espenscheid

Rides	*Ilo Orleans*	8
Lou Stick, Hunter	*Gertrude Crampton*	10
Rabbit Tale	*Rowena Bennett*	12
Hi! Ho! Three in a Row	*Louise Woodcock*	14
Pretending	*Alice and Martin Provensen*	18
The Wee Little House	*Patricia Scarry*	20

GOING SOMEWHERE

Illustrated by Paul Granger

A Sack of Potatoes	*Rita S. Cooper*	24
A Birthday for Susan	*Eva Knox Evans*	28
The Weather Story	*Margaret Wise Brown*	34
Singing-Time	*Rose Fyleman*	36
Susan Blue	*Kate Greenaway*	36

The Big, Big World   *Marion Conger*   37

The Wonderful Feast   *Esphyr Slobodkina*   43

The Barnyard   *Maude Burnham*   46

The Dog and the Rooster   *Old Tale*   48

I Went for a Walk   *Lois Lenski*   52

OUT IN THE OPEN
Illustrated by Harold Berson

A Cowboy's Day   *Clyde Robert Bulla*   54

The Wild White Horse   *Retold by Willis Lindquist*   60

The Story That Never Ends   *Folklore*   64

Little Star   *Elizabeth Beecher*   65

How the Chipmunk Got His Stripes
Retold by Willis Lindquist   71

How the Bear Lost His Tail *Retold by Leland B. Jacobs*   73

CLEVER ANIMALS
Illustrated by Susan Perl

Wonderful Willy   *Tony Brice*   78

The Mouse's House   *Pat Day*   84

Muddy Mouse   *Helen and Alf Evers*   86

Bird Talk   *Aileen Fisher*   91

One Cold Day   *Elizabeth Coatsworth*   92

The Fox and His Bag   *Old Tale*   96

Angus and the Ducks   *Marjorie Flack*   103

The Old Woman and Her Pig   *Old Tale*   109

Homes   *Ilo Orleans*   116

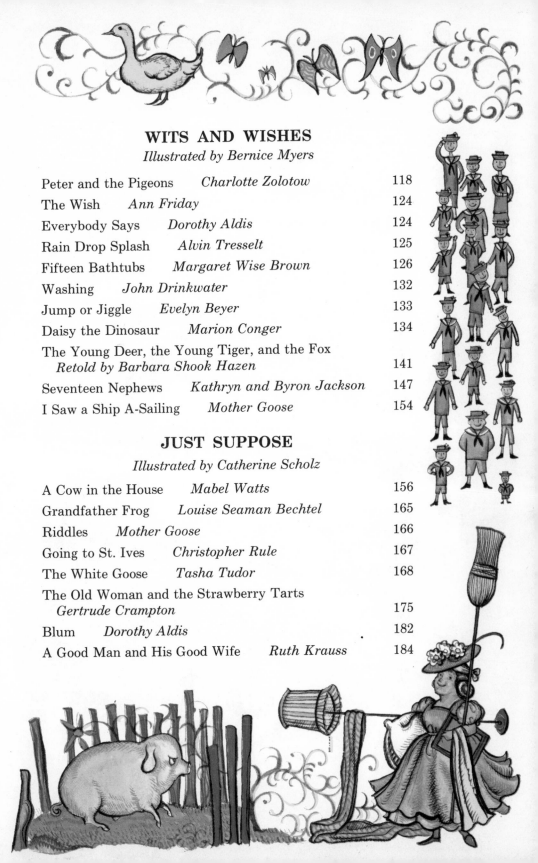

WITS AND WISHES
Illustrated by Bernice Myers

Peter and the Pigeons   *Charlotte Zolotow*   118

The Wish   *Ann Friday*   124

Everybody Says   *Dorothy Aldis*   124

Rain Drop Splash   *Alvin Tresselt*   125

Fifteen Bathtubs   *Margaret Wise Brown*   126

Washing   *John Drinkwater*   132

Jump or Jiggle   *Evelyn Beyer*   133

Daisy the Dinosaur   *Marion Conger*   134

The Young Deer, the Young Tiger, and the Fox
Retold by Barbara Shook Hazen   141

Seventeen Nephews   *Kathryn and Byron Jackson*   147

I Saw a Ship A-Sailing   *Mother Goose*   154

JUST SUPPOSE
Illustrated by Catherine Scholz

A Cow in the House   *Mabel Watts*   156

Grandfather Frog   *Louise Seaman Bechtel*   165

Riddles   *Mother Goose*   166

Going to St. Ives   *Christopher Rule*   167

The White Goose   *Tasha Tudor*   168

The Old Woman and the Strawberry Tarts
Gertrude Crampton   175

Blum   *Dorothy Aldis*   182

A Good Man and His Good Wife   *Ruth Krauss*   184

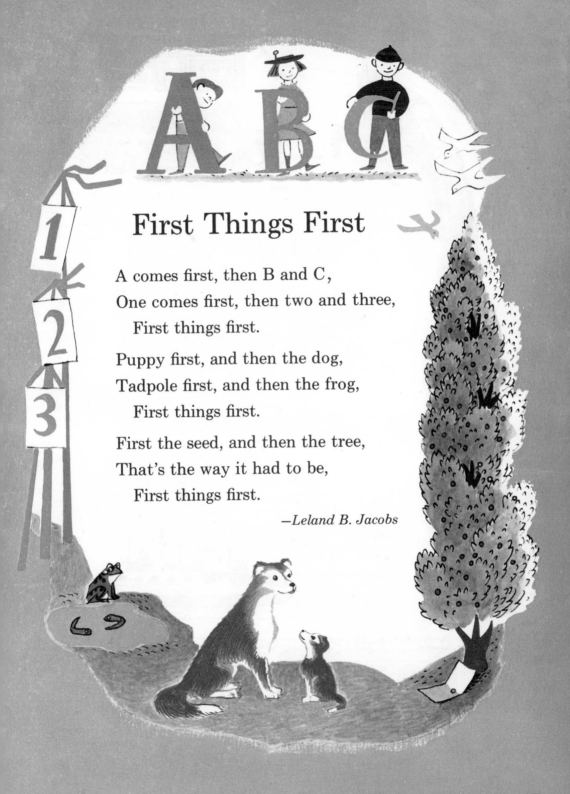

First Things First

A comes first, then B and C,
One comes first, then two and three,
  First things first.

Puppy first, and then the dog,
Tadpole first, and then the frog,
  First things first.

First the seed, and then the tree,
That's the way it had to be,
  First things first.

           —*Leland B. Jacobs*

7

Rides

I ride on a bus.
I ride on a train.
I ride on a trolley.
I ride on a plane.
I ride on a ferry.
I ride in a car.

I ride on my skates—
But not very far.
But, best of all,
The ride I like
Is 'round the block
On my new bike.

Ilo Orleans

9

Lou Stick, Hunter

Gertrude Crampton

"I am a hunter," says Lou Stick.
"I am brave and strong and mighty.
"I will shoot a bear for breakfast.

"Well, I will shoot a deer
for breakfast.

"Who wants deer? I will shoot
a rabbit for breakfast.

"I am very fond of oatmeal
for breakfast," says Lou.

Rabbit Tale

A rabbit sat inside a hat.
He was not thin. He was not fat.
He nibbled this. He nibbled that.
He sat and sat and sat and sat.

There was a dog. There was a cat.
They saw the rabbit in the hat.
The rabbit said, "I don't like that."

He ran and ran, and found a log.
He hid from cat. He hid from dog.
He hid inside the hollow log.
And there he sat and sat and sat.

He said, "I'm safe from dog and cat.
I like this better than a hat."
And that was that.

Rowena Bennett

Hi! Ho! Three in a Row

Hi! Ho!
Three girls in a row,
Joan and Susie and Ann.
  Susie has shoes,
    And Joan has a bow.
Then which do you think is Ann?

Hi! Ho!
Three boys in a row,
Dan and Billy and Joe.
  Bill has a boat,
    And Joe wears a coat.
Then which of the boys is Dan?
  Do you know?

Rum-tumpty-tum!
Who's beating that drum?
Wally or Dick or Paul?
  Dick is blowing a trumpet (toot!).
  Wally is trying to play a flute.
Who can be making
    that nice tum-tum,
That fine, loud rum-tum-tum?

"High! High!
Let's climb to the sky!"
Say Don and Barbie and Kate.
  Barbie's climbed highest,
  And Don is the lowest.
Then where shall we look for Kate?

Hi! Ho!
Three dogs in a row,
Tuck and Sammy and Jip.
 Tuck wears a collar,
 Sammy has spots.
Now can you tell which is Jip?
 Can you tell which is Jip?

Scurry! Scurry!
Three cats in a hurry,
Dorcas, Tabby, and Puss.
 Tabby has stripes,
 And Puss is all white,
 But Dorcas is black
 as a rainy night.
Can you tell which is which,
 Dorcas, Tabby, and Puss?

Rub-a-dub-dub!
Three pets in a tub,
A frog, a turtle, a fish.
  Flatty's the turtle,
  And Croaky's the frog.
Then who do you think is named
    Swish?
  And why do they call him Swish?

Oh! Oh!
Three flowers aglow,
A clover, a poppy, a rose.
  The bee's on the clover,
  The poppy bends over.
Can anyone find a rose, a rose?
  I wonder which one is the rose.
Three in a row—which do you know?

Louise Woodcock

Pretending

I have quite a handy habit.
When I hurry, I'm a rabbit.

When I'm buying chops and stew,
I'm a tiger—hungry, too!

When I meet a friendly horse,
I'm another horse, of course.

If you run and try to catch me,
I will vanish in the air.
And before you finish blinking,
I'm a most surprising bear.

So, if when you go out walking,
There's a fox behind a tree,
Don't be afraid and call for aid,
It's really only me.

Alice and Martin Provensen

The Wee Little House

Patricia Scarry

A wee little house sits alone
in the woods.
  In the house lives a wee little man.
  "I live all alone," says
the wee little man.
  But he only thinks he does.

In a tiny hole, in the wee little
house, lives a fat little,
gray little mouse.

And nobody knows that he lives
there—nobody else but the mouse.

Just under the roof live three gray
squirrels.

By the window is a robin's nest.

Snug under the step is
a fat raccoon.

And under the porch a small rabbit
lives.

Yes, they all have homes
in the wee little house.

But the wee little man
never sees them.

And the wee little man
never hears them.

"I live all alone," says
the wee little man.

But he only thinks he does.

Going Somewhere

Let's go somewhere!
  Where shall it be?
Out beyond the moon and stars?
  Far across the sea?

Let's go somewhere
  Not so far away,
The park, or hill, or any place
  Where we can run and play.

—*Leland B. Jacobs*

A Sack of Potatoes

Rita S. Cooper

One very bright morning
Joe Jones came down the street
bumping a sack of potatoes
very close to his feet.
Joe skipped and he jumped,
right over a hump,
and suddenly, *thump!*
The sack dumped—
and out rolled the potatoes!
They rolled and they rolled and
they rolled, bumpety, bump, bump.

 From the book BELIEVE AND MAKE-BELIEVE by Lucy Sprague Mitchell and Irma Black. Copyright 1956 by the Bank Street of Education. Published by E. P. Dutton & Co., Inc. and reprinted with their permission.

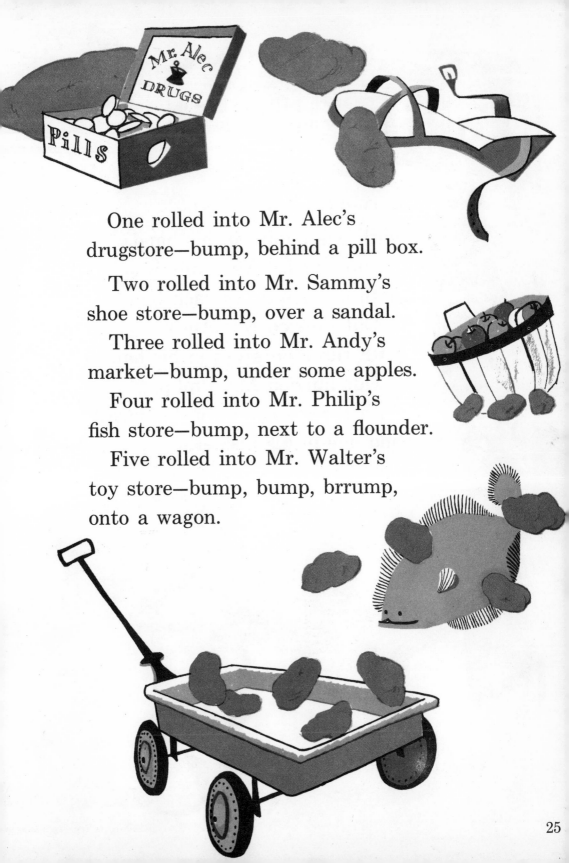

One rolled into Mr. Alec's
drugstore—bump, behind a pill box.

Two rolled into Mr. Sammy's
shoe store—bump, over a sandal.

Three rolled into Mr. Andy's
market—bump, under some apples.

Four rolled into Mr. Philip's
fish store—bump, next to a flounder.

Five rolled into Mr. Walter's
toy store—bump, bump, brrump,
onto a wagon.

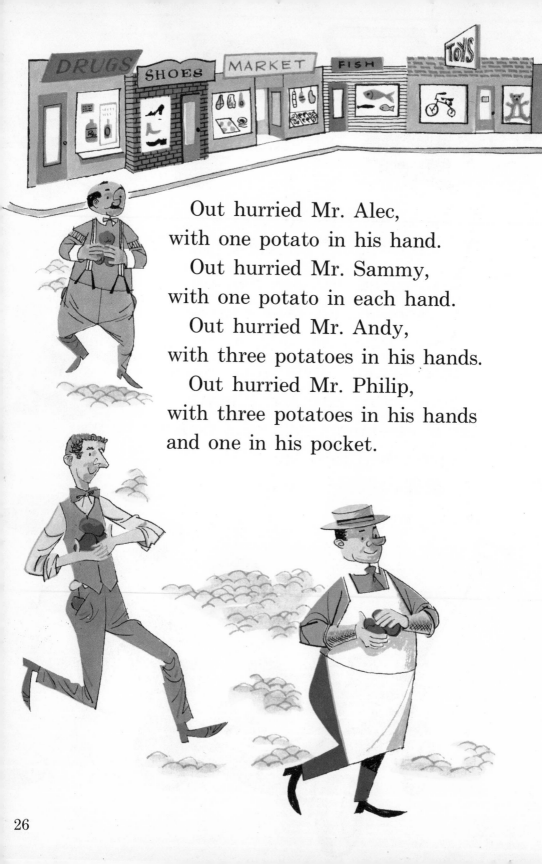

Out hurried Mr. Alec,
with one potato in his hand.
Out hurried Mr. Sammy,
with one potato in each hand.
Out hurried Mr. Andy,
with three potatoes in his hands.
Out hurried Mr. Philip,
with three potatoes in his hands
and one in his pocket.

Out hurried Mr. Walter,
with three potatoes in his hands
and two in his pockets.

Joe sang, "Oh, there they are!"
and stuffed them back into the sack,
one after the other.

And down the street he went
with the sack of potatoes
bumping very close to his feet,
that very bright morning.

A Birthday for Susan

Eva Knox Evans

It was Susan's birthday.

"What will I get for my birthday?" asked Susan.

"A surprise," said Mother. "You must wait."

While Susan was waiting, she went for a walk. She walked until she met a man in a gray suit. He was not singing a tune. He was not dancing a jig. He was walking.

"What do you carry in your big gray bag?" asked Susan politely.

"Mail," said the man. "I carry mail." Susan looked, and there was

U. S. MAIL

on the side of the bag.

"I know," said Susan. "You are the mailman."

Susan walked a little more. She
walked and she walked until she saw
a big truck.

The truck was not dancing a jig.
It was not running a race. It was
standing by the sidewalk.

"What do you carry in your truck?"
asked Susan politely.

"Parcels," said the man
in the truck. "I deliver parcels."

Susan looked, and there was

PARCELS

on the side of the truck.

"I know," said Susan. "You are
the parcel man."

Susan walked a little more
until she heard a noise. It was not
a boom-boom noise. It was not
a bim-bam noise. It was
a ting-a-ling noise.

Susan looked and saw a bicycle.
It was not like Susan's bicycle.

It was a white bicycle with a big
white box on the front. Susan did not
have to ask what was in the white
box. Something was printed on the
side of the box. It said,

ICE CREAM

"I know, I know," said Susan.
"You are the ice-cream man."

It was time for Susan to go home.
She went home singing a tune. She
went home dancing a jig. She went
home running a race. And there she
was at home!

"Surprise!" said Mother.

There were four letters for Susan.
There were one, two, three, four
birthday letters for Susan!

"The mailman delivered them,"
said Mother.

"Oh," said Susan, very surprised.
"The mailman had something
in his big gray bag for me!"

"Surprise!" said Mother.

There was a parcel for Susan.

It was a birthday doll.

"The parcel man delivered it,"
said Mother.

"Oh, my," said Susan, so surprised.
"The parcel man had something
for me, too!"

"Here is another surprise,"
said Mother.

"Ice cream!" said Susan.
"The ice-cream man had ice cream
in the big white box for me."

And a birthday cake! There were
candles on the cake and writing that
said,

HAPPY BIRTHDAY !

Mother had made the cake.
"Not one surprise, but
four surprises," said Susan.
"What a happy birthday!"

The Weather Story

Snow falls down
And covers the ground,
And where is the boy
who is walking?

The sun shines hot
On a sunny spot,
And where is the boy
who is walking?

Fog drifts in from over the sea,
Gray and soft and quietly,
And where is the boy
who is walking?

 From "The Little Weather Story" in READ ME ANOTHER STORY, compiled by the Child Study Association of America. Copyrig 1949 by Thomas Y. Crowell Company, New York, publishers.

The sunset reddens the evening sky,
Reddens the barn and the old pigsty,
And where is the boy
who is walking?

The night comes softly all around,
Dark in the sky and dark
on the ground,
And *here* is the boy who is walking.

Margaret Wise Brown

Singing-Time

I wake in the morning early
And always, the very first thing,
I poke out my head and
  I sit up in bed
And I sing and I sing and I sing.

Rose Fyleman

Susan Blue

Oh, Susan Blue,
  How do you do?
Please may I go for a walk with you?
  Where shall we go?
  Oh, I know—
Down in the meadow
  Where the cowslips grow!

Kate Greenaway

"Singing-Time" from THE FAIRY GREEN by Rose Fyleman. Copyright 1923 by Doubleday & Company, Inc. Reprinted by permission of the publishers and of The Society of Authors, London.

The Big, Big World

Marion Conger

One day after school Chip set out
to see the world.

He followed his feet to the end
of the street and came to a meadow.

"Hello," said Chip to a rabbit
in the meadow. "Which way do I go
to see the world?"

"This meadow is world enough
for me," said the rabbit. "Follow
your nose if you want to see more."

In the meadow Chip picked a blade
of grass to chew on. He picked
some sweet clover for his mother.

Then he followed his nose till he
came to a farm.

"Hello," said Chip to a goose
in the farmyard. "Which way do I go
to see the world?"

"This farm is world enough
for me," said the goose, shaking
its feathers. "Follow the wind
if you want to see more."

Chip wet his finger and held it up
to see which way the wind was
blowing. He picked up a white goose
feather and put it in his pocket.

Then he followed the wind. He
followed it till he came to a brook.

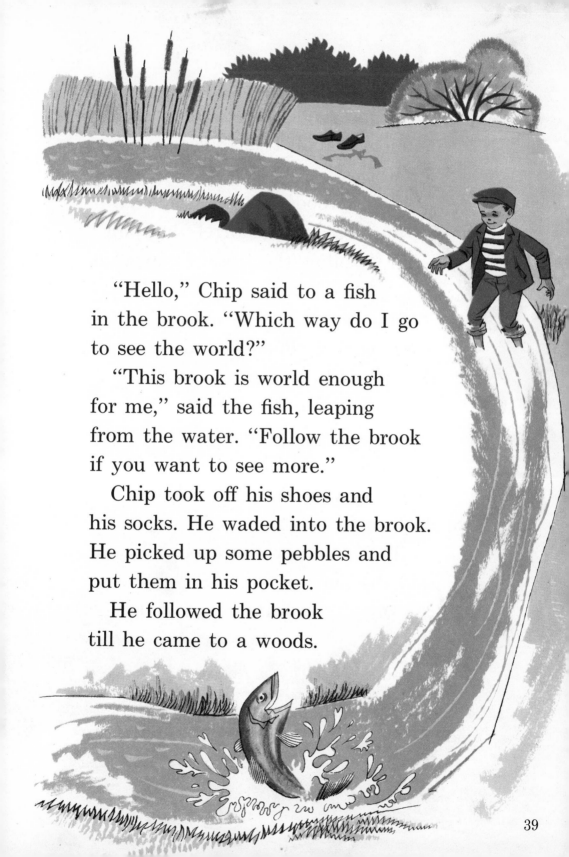

"Hello," Chip said to a fish
in the brook. "Which way do I go
to see the world?"

"This brook is world enough
for me," said the fish, leaping
from the water. "Follow the brook
if you want to see more."

Chip took off his shoes and
his socks. He waded into the brook.
He picked up some pebbles and
put them in his pocket.

He followed the brook
till he came to a woods.

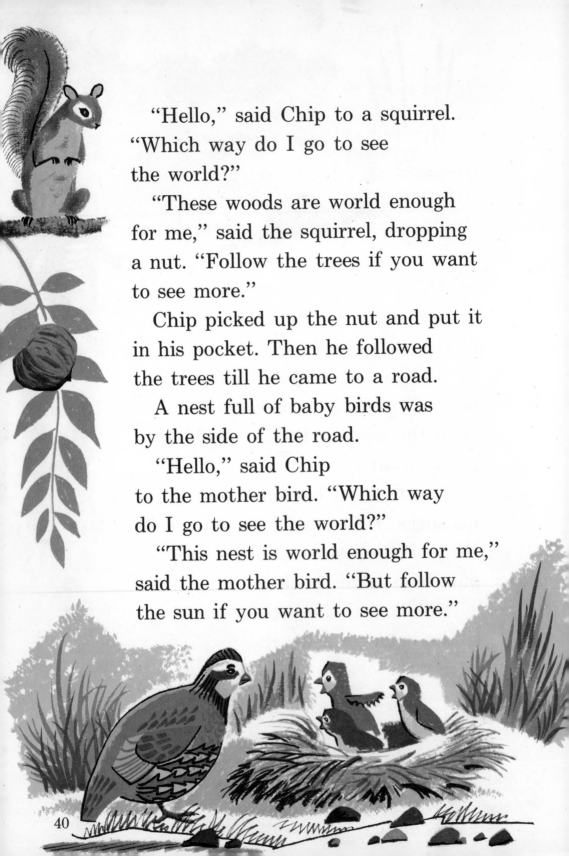

"Hello," said Chip to a squirrel.
"Which way do I go to see
the world?"

"These woods are world enough
for me," said the squirrel, dropping
a nut. "Follow the trees if you want
to see more."

Chip picked up the nut and put it
in his pocket. Then he followed
the trees till he came to a road.

A nest full of baby birds was
by the side of the road.

"Hello," said Chip
to the mother bird. "Which way
do I go to see the world?"

"This nest is world enough for me,"
said the mother bird. "But follow
the sun if you want to see more."

Chip picked a red berry from the
bush and put it in his pocket. Then
he followed the sun down the road.

The sun was getting lower and
lower and lower in the sky. And Chip
was getting hungrier and hungrier and
hungrier. The world seemed like
a very big place indeed.

Then the sun began to sink
behind the hills. Chip hurried.
He followed the sinking sun
till he came to a street.

Down the street came the smell
of fried chicken. Chip followed
the smell to his own house.

"Hello," said Chip's mother. "Where have you been? It is almost dark."

"I have been out to see the world," said Chip. "It is a very big place."

Chip put his hand in his pocket. "I found many things in the big world," said Chip. "I have clover from the meadow, and a feather from a goose, and some pebbles from the brook. I have a nut from the woods and a red berry from a bush. They are all for you!"

"What beautiful gifts!" said Chip's mother. Then she said, "You must be very hungry after your trip."

And, of course, Chip was very hungry after such a long trip.

The Wonderful Feast

Esphyr Slobodkina

Early in the morning, Farmer Jones got up and said, "It is a beautiful morning. The sun is shining bright. The birds are singing, and I feel fine!"

Then he went into the barn and gave his horse a great big breakfast.

"My," said the old horse. "What a wonderful feast I'm going to have!"

He ate all he wanted and went to sleep. Then everything was quiet again.

A goat came into the barn.
She looked at what was left
of the horse's meal.

"My, oh, my!" she said. "What
a wonderful feast I'm going to have!"

She ate all she wanted and left
the barn.

Just then the hen came in
looking for breakfast.

"Children, children," she called.
"Look what a wonderful feast we are
going to have!"

In a moment the floor was covered
with little chicks, having

their breakfast.

All was quiet again in the barn
after they left.

"Oh, my—oh, my—oh, my!"
whispered a little mouse, peeping out
of his hole. "What a wonderful feast
I'm going to have!"

He crossed the floor to where
the grains lay and took all he could
to his house.

Then a busy old ant came into
the barn. He picked up the last grain
and took it away. "My, oh, my!" said
the ant. "What a wonderful feast
I'm going to have!"

The Barnyard

When the farmer's day is done,
In the barnyard, every one,
Beast and bird politely say,
"Thank you for my food today."
The cow says, "Moo!"
The pigeon, "Coo!"
The sheep says, "Baa!"
The lamb says, "Maa!"
The hen, "Cluck! Cluck!"

"Quack!" says the duck.
The dog, "Bow-wow!"
The cat, "Meow!"
The horse says, "Neigh!
I love sweet hay!"
The pig near by
Grunts in his sty.
When the barn is locked up tight,
Then the farmer says, "Good night,"
Thanks his animals, every one,
For the work that has been done.

Maude Burnham

The Dog and the Rooster

Old Tale

One day a dog and a rooster who were very good friends started out to see the world. Before they had gone very far, it began to grow dark.

"Let us stay here for the night," said the rooster. "I can roost on the lowest branch of this tree, and you can sleep in the hollow trunk."

"That will be fine," said the dog.

So the rooster flew up to his branch, and the dog curled up in his hole. They both went to sleep.

48

In the morning the rooster woke up
early and began to crow,
"Cock-a-doodle-do! Cock-a-doodle-do!"

A fox off in the woods heard him.

"That is a rooster crowing," the fox
said to himself. "He will make
a fine breakfast for me."

So the fox followed the sound
of the crowing. Soon he could see
the rooster up in the tree.

"Cock-a-doodle-do!" said the rooster.

"Ha, what a fine breakfast he will be
for me!" said the fox. "Now I must
make him come down from that tree."

SCHOOL DISTRICT #49

So the fox said to the rooster,
"What a fine rooster you are! How
well you crow! Will you come
to my house for breakfast?"

"Thank you," said the rooster.
"I will be glad to come if my friend
may come, too."

The fox was pleased. Now he would
have two fine roosters to eat!

"Oh, yes," said the fox. "I will be glad to have your friend come. Where is he?"

"My friend is sleeping in the trunk of this tree," said the rooster. "Just wake him up."

"Oh, this is fine," thought the fox.

So he put his head into the hole in the tree trunk and said, "Will you come to my house for breakfast?"

"Yes," said the dog. Then out he jumped and caught the fox by the nose.

I Went for a Walk

I went for a walk
And what did I see?
The sun in the sky
Shining down on me.

Houses in yards
All along the way,
People on the sidewalk,
Happy and gay.

A woman walked by,
A man came too;
A dog wagged his tail,
A cat said mew.

Everybody smiled,
Happy as could be,
Going for a walk—
Just like me!

Lois Lenski

52

Copyright 1947 by Lois Lenski. Reprinted by permission of the author from I WENT FOR A WALK, A Read-and-Sing Book, © 1958 by Lois Lenski, published by Henry Z. Walck, Inc.

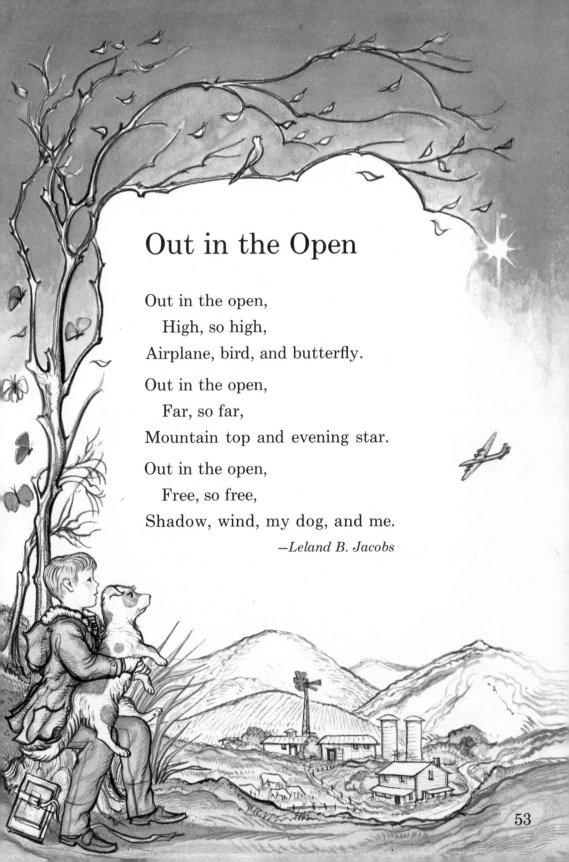

Out in the Open

Out in the open,
  High, so high,
Airplane, bird, and butterfly.

Out in the open,
  Far, so far,
Mountain top and evening star.

Out in the open,
  Free, so free,
Shadow, wind, my dog, and me.

—Leland B. Jacobs

53

A Cowboy's Day

Clyde Robert Bulla

Danny was visiting Uncle Mack's ranch. There were six cowboys on the ranch. One of them was named Slim. He had red hair and freckles.

Danny asked Slim, "What does a cowboy do all day?"

Slim said, "You can ride with me tomorrow. You can see what a cowboy does all day."

The next morning Slim rode a white horse. Danny rode a spotted pony. Shep, the collie dog, ran with them.

From SURPRISE FOR A COWBOY. Copyright 1950 by the author, Clyde Robert Bulla. Thomas Y. Crowell Company, New York, publishers.

"Where are we going?" asked
Danny.

"We are going to drive some cattle
to the mountains, where the grass is
green," said Slim.

They rode over a hill. At the foot
of the hill was a water hole. All around
the water hole were white-faced cattle.

"Hey! Hey!" shouted Slim. "Get
along there." Shep barked, and
the cattle began to move away from
the water hole.

The mountains did not look
far away, but it was nearly dark
when they got there.

"This is a good place for the cattle,"
said Slim. "It has plenty of grass and
water. We'll camp here tonight."

Danny looked around. He saw a log
cabin under the trees. They tied their
horses under the trees and went into
the cabin. In the cabin were a stove
and a wood box, a table, and two bunks.

"This is a cow camp," said Slim.
"When a cowboy is riding the range,
he stops at a cow camp. We keep
something to eat here. We'll have
a good supper tonight."

After supper, they took off their
boots and went to bed. Shep slept
under one of the bunks.

In the morning they had an early
breakfast. Then they cleaned the cabin.
Slim cut some wood, and Danny
filled the wood box.

"Now everything is ready for the
next cowboy," said Slim. "Today we
will fix fences on our way back home."
They rode away from the camp. Shep
ran after them.

"What else does a cowboy do?"
Danny asked.

Slim said, "A cowboy does many
things. He takes care of his horses.
He ropes calves and brands them.
Sometimes he shoots a snake."

They rode slowly along the trail.
They found several places where the
fences were broken. Slim stopped to
fix the broken places.

At the bottom of a hill Shep began to bark. Danny looked around. He saw some trees and a pile of rocks.

Danny called, "Slim! A little calf is caught between two big rocks."

Slim came quickly. He moved the rocks. The calf was free, but it could not walk. Slim ran his hand over the calf's leg. "No bones are broken. It was caught in the rocks so long that the feeling has gone out of its foot."

Slim pointed to the brand on the calf. "This is not one of our calves," he said. "It belongs to the Circle-A Ranch. We can stop there on the way home." He showed Danny how to carry the calf on his pony.

They rode until they came to the
Circle-A Ranch. Dogs barked,
and a boy ran out of the house.

"That's my pet calf, Trixie," said
the boy. "Where did you find her?"

"We found her on our ranch,"
said Danny. "Her foot was caught
in the rocks."

The boy took the calf in his arms.
He said, "Thank you for saving
Trixie."

Danny said, "Don't thank me.
Thank Shep. He found the calf
in the rocks."

The Wild White Horse

Retold by Willis Lindquist

At night cowboys like to sit around
a campfire and sing and tell stories.
One of the stories they often tell is
about a wild white horse.

A wild horse it was, with silvery
mane and tail, and it could run faster
than the wind.

A big horse, and smart—and the
most beautiful horse in the world,
cowboys said. Each one that saw
it wanted it for his own.

One cowboy named Tex almost did catch the white horse.

He watched and waited, and one day he saw the horse drinking from a pool. It was a deep pool of spring water.

Tex built a fence around that pool, and he left the gate wide open. Then he hid, and he waited.

But the beautiful white horse was too smart. It saw the fence, and it stopped going to that water hole.

Tex waited. The dry season came, and all the water holes dried up—all except that one, which was fed by springs. Tex waited, for he knew the white horse would soon have to come there to drink.

At last, one day, the horse did
come to the pool. It went right inside
the fence. Tex quickly shut the gate.
Then he gave a whoop—the white
horse was his at last!

The sun had set, and Tex knew that
it was too dark to rope the horse that
night. He would have to wait until
morning.

But in the morning the horse had
gone. The great, strong horse had
smashed right through the gate!

Sadly, Tex turned away.

Many cowboys had tried to catch
the wild horse before, and many more
tried after Tex.

But to this day, no one has caught
the beautiful white horse. Free
and wild it runs—faster than the wind.

The Story That Never Ends

It was a dark and stormy night.
Some Indians were sitting around the
campfire. Their chief rose and said . . .

It was a dark and stormy night.
Some Indians were sitting around the
campfire. Their chief rose and said . . .

It was a dark and stormy night.
Some Indians were sitting around the
campfire. Their chief rose and said . . .

Little Star

Elizabeth Beecher

Little Star was an Indian boy. His
full name was Great-Star-in-the-Sky.
But everybody on the Canyon
Ranch called him Little Star.

One evening Little Star heard Bill
Allen talking to one of the cowboys.

"Happy, we'll brand the calves
on the north range tomorrow,"
said Bill. "Tell the boys to be
ready to ride at sun-up."

"Okay," said Happy, the cowboy,
starting for the bunkhouse.

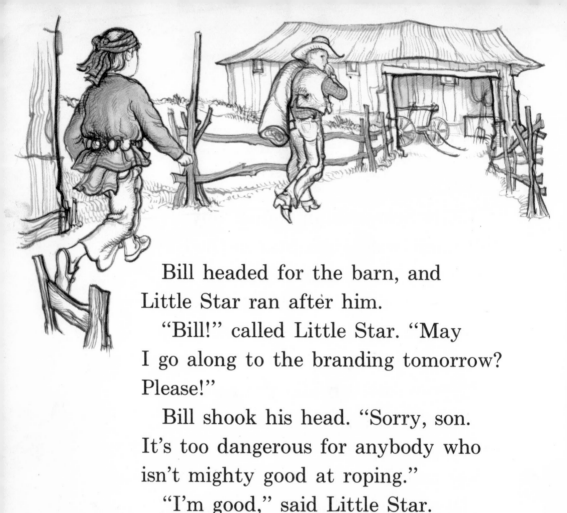

Bill headed for the barn, and
Little Star ran after him.

"Bill!" called Little Star. "May
I go along to the branding tomorrow?
Please!"

Bill shook his head. "Sorry, son.
It's too dangerous for anybody who
isn't mighty good at roping."

"I'm good," said Little Star.

Again Bill shook his head.

So Little Star sadly walked away.

By sun-up next morning,
Little Star was no longer sad.

He hurried to the corral where the
cowboys were saddling their horses.
Perching on the top of the fence,
he tried to rope their saddle horns.
But all he roped was Happy's hat.

Happy lifted Little Star off the
fence. "You need a good spanking,
little fellow!" he said.

Little Star raced for a tall tree.
He stayed up in the tree until Happy
and Bill and the boys rode off toward
the north range.

Then he slid down and got his rope.
He mounted Clover, his little burro,
and rode after them.

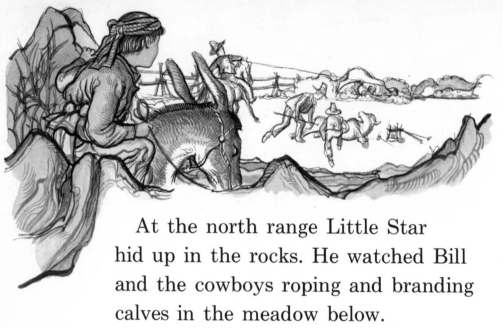

At the north range Little Star
hid up in the rocks. He watched Bill
and the cowboys roping and branding
calves in the meadow below.

Suddenly a calf broke away and
headed straight for Little Star's
hiding place.

Little Star shook out his rope and
waited until the calf came alongside.
He swung his rope right over the
calf's head.

Quickly Little Star pulled the rope tight. But the calf squirmed and twisted and tugged until he pulled Little Star off Clover's back!

Little Star did not let go of the rope.

Soon Bill rode by. His rope flew through the air—and caught that calf!

Happy rode up and took the calf back to the branding fire.

Bill smiled down at Little Star. "That was good roping," he said.

Little Star smiled. He knew that now he could stay at the branding. Then he stopped smiling.

"But, Bill, I'm not really a very good roper," he said. "I let the calf pull me right off Clover's back."

"Don't worry about that," chuckled Bill. "If I hired only cowboys who'd never taken a spill, nobody would be working for me—not even myself!"

How the Chipmunk Got His Stripes

An Old Indian Legend
Retold by Willis Lindquist

Long ago, all the birds and animals
met to decide how much light they
should have.

"I think we should have light
all the time," said Eagle.

"No," said Owl. "Light hurts our
eyes. It should be dark all the time."

"No, no!" shouted many animals.

"Owl is right," said Bear. "Hunting
is better in the dark. It should always
be dark."

Then Chipmunk said, "I think
half the day should be dark and
the other half should be light."

The other animals thought
Chipmunk had the best idea. So they
divided the day into a light part and
a dark part.

But Bear wanted it all dark. He was
so angry at Chipmunk that he chased
him. Before Chipmunk could reach his
hole, Bear clawed his back, leaving
long scratches.

From that day to this, all chipmunks
have had long stripes on their backs.

How the Bear Lost His Tail

Retold by Leland B. Jacobs

Mr. Fox lived in the forest.
All the forest animals knew him.
They knew he was sly. They knew he
played jokes on everybody.

Mr. Bear lived in the forest, too.
All the forest animals knew him.
They knew he was slow. They knew
he was honest. They knew he trusted
everybody.

One winter morning Mr. Bear met
Mr. Fox. Mr. Fox was carrying
a big fish.

Mr. Bear was hungry. He had not
had breakfast. He wanted
a big fish, too.

"What a big fish!" said Mr. Bear.

"Yes, it is a big fish," said Mr. Fox.

"Did you buy it?" asked Mr. Bear.

"No, I caught it," said Mr. Fox.

"I'm hungry," said Mr. Bear. "Could
I catch a fish?"

"Of course you could," said Mr. Fox.
"I'll tell you how. Go to the river.
Cut a hole in the ice. Put your tail
in the hole. Catch a fish on your tail."

Mr. Bear went to the river. He cut
a hole in the ice. He put his tail
in the hole. He sat and sat and sat.
He was hungry.

He sat and sat some more. He was
cold. He sat and sat some more. He
was tired and sleepy. He sat and sat
some more. But Mr. Bear caught no
fish.

Mr. Bear was very tired. He was
very cold. He was very sleepy. He was
very hungry. But he had caught not
one fish.

"I won't sit here any more," said
Mr. Bear. He tried to get up. He was
frozen fast. His tail was frozen
in the ice.

Poor Mr. Bear! He pulled gently.
He pulled harder and harder and
harder. He was still frozen fast.

Then he gave a great jerk. He was
free. But his tail was still frozen
in the ice.

To this day, bears don't trust
foxes. And all bears have
short, small, stubby, stumpy tails.

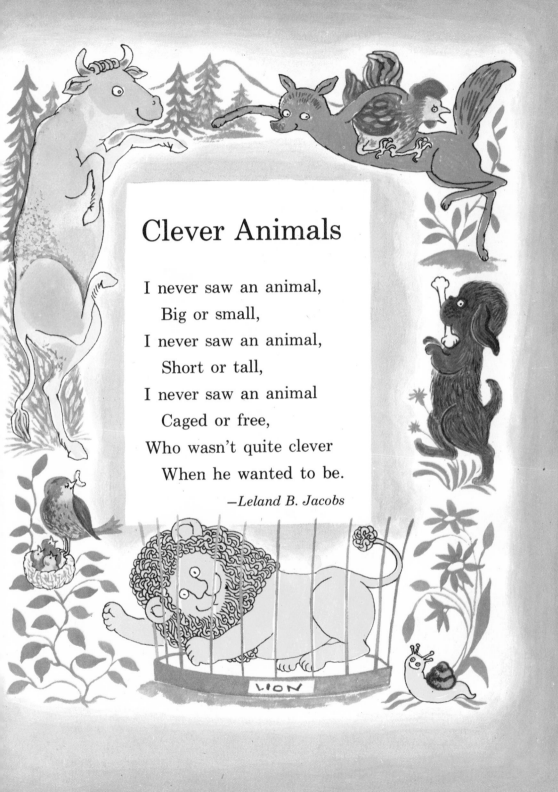

Clever Animals

I never saw an animal,
 Big or small,
I never saw an animal,
 Short or tall,
I never saw an animal
 Caged or free,
Who wasn't quite clever
 When he wanted to be.

—*Leland B. Jacobs*

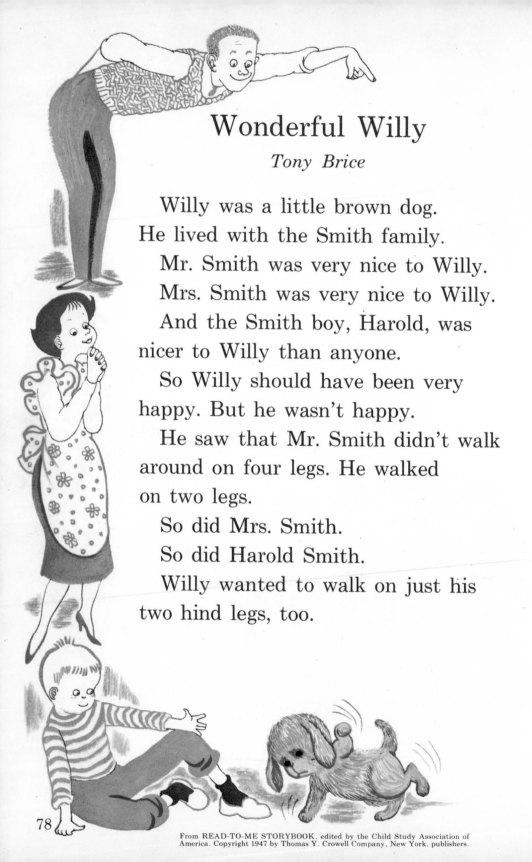

Wonderful Willy

Tony Brice

Willy was a little brown dog.
He lived with the Smith family.
Mr. Smith was very nice to Willy.
Mrs. Smith was very nice to Willy.
And the Smith boy, Harold, was
nicer to Willy than anyone.
So Willy should have been very
happy. But he wasn't happy.
He saw that Mr. Smith didn't walk
around on four legs. He walked
on two legs.
So did Mrs. Smith.
So did Harold Smith.
Willy wanted to walk on just his
two hind legs, too.

78

From READ-TO-ME STORYBOOK, edited by the Child Study Association of
America. Copyright 1947 by Thomas Y. Crowell Company, New York, publishers.

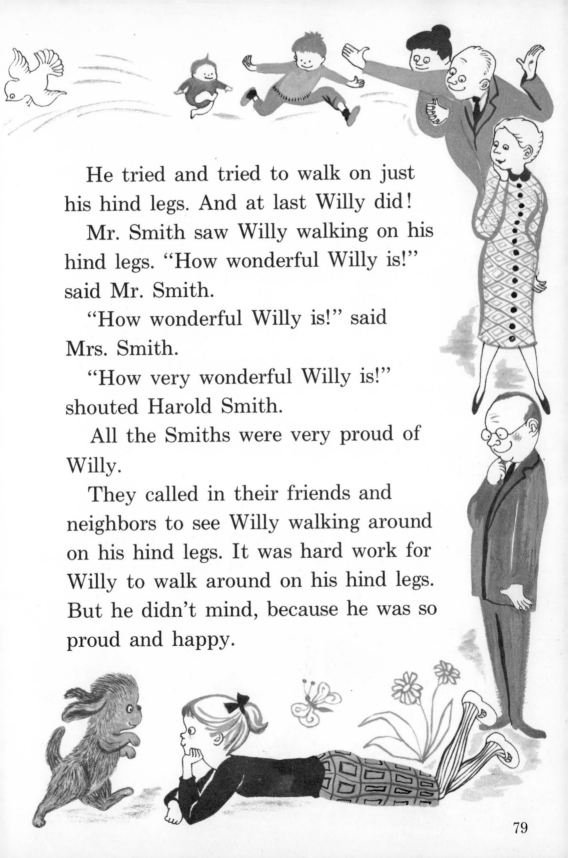

He tried and tried to walk on just his hind legs. And at last Willy did!

Mr. Smith saw Willy walking on his hind legs. "How wonderful Willy is!" said Mr. Smith.

"How wonderful Willy is!" said Mrs. Smith.

"How very wonderful Willy is!" shouted Harold Smith.

All the Smiths were very proud of Willy.

They called in their friends and neighbors to see Willy walking around on his hind legs. It was hard work for Willy to walk around on his hind legs. But he didn't mind, because he was so proud and happy.

One day the Smiths were shopping on Main Street. Willy walked with them, on his hind legs.

Everybody who came along stopped to admire the way Willy walked on two legs. They all thought he was wonderful.

Just then the kind butcher came out of his shop. He put some bones down on the sidewalk for the dogs.

Dogs came running from everywhere—old dogs, young dogs, black dogs, white dogs, brown dogs, yellow dogs, and spotted dogs! Even a little puppy, who wasn't old enough to eat a bone, ran to the butcher shop.

Willy tried to run on his hind legs. But he couldn't. He could only walk slowly.

He wanted a bone so much that at last he dropped down on all four legs and *ran*.

It felt so good to be on four legs again that Willy ran faster than he had ever run before. He ran so fast that he reached the butcher shop first and picked out the biggest bone of all.

When Willy had eaten his bone,
he started back to the Smiths. He
remembered how proud of him
Mr. and Mrs. Smith had been when
he walked on just his hind legs.

Willy remembered how very proud
Harold Smith had been.

Poor Willy thought the Smiths
would be ashamed of him. He had
stopped walking on two legs and had
run on all four! And right on Main
Street in front of all their friends, too!

Willy walked very slowly, with his
tail between his legs. He felt very
unhappy.

But when Mr. Smith saw Willy, he
said, "How wonderful Willy is! He can
walk on just his hind legs when he
wants to. But when he wants to go
fast, he can run faster on all four legs
than any other dog."

"How wonderful Willy is!" said
Mrs. Smith, too.

"How *very* wonderful Willy is!"
shouted Harold Smith.

And from that day on, when Willy
walked on his two hind legs, he felt
happy.

When he ran on all four legs, he
felt happy.

But when he just sat by the fire
with Harold Smith, he felt *very*
happy.

The Mouse's House

One time there was a woodland mouse
Who lived inside a funny house.
It had no doors,
It had no floors,
The home of Mister Mouse.

The mouse's house was full of weeds,
And bits of grass, and little seeds.
There were no chairs,
There were no stairs,
And yet it seemed to suit his needs.

The little mousies had no bed,
There was no roof top overhead.
There was no clock,
There was no lock,
No lamp (they used the sun instead).

No roof, no lock, no clock, no doors,
No bed, no chairs, no stairs, no floors,
Where was the house
Of Mister Mouse?
Why, in a grassy field outdoors!

Pat Day

Muddy Mouse

Helen and Alf Evers

Every day the Mouse family went for a walk.

When they came to a mud puddle, Father Mouse walked around it. Mother Mouse walked around it. Sister Mouse and Brother Mouse walked around it, too. But little Muddy Mouse walked right through it. He liked mud.

His friend, the horse, didn't like mud. The cow didn't like mud. The dog and the cat didn't like mud. But Muddy Mouse liked mud so much that he cried when there wasn't any.

From READ-TO-ME STORYBOOK, compiled by the Child Study Association of America. Copyright 1947 by Thomas Y. Crowell Company, New York, publishers.

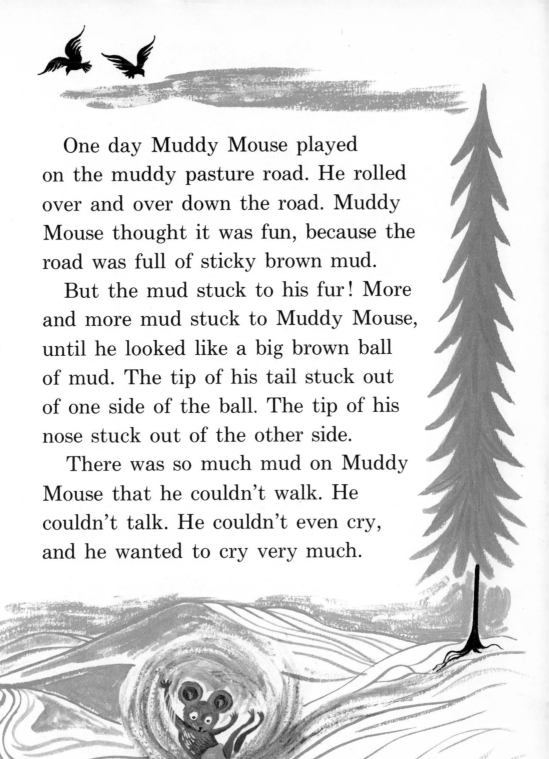

One day Muddy Mouse played
on the muddy pasture road. He rolled
over and over down the road. Muddy
Mouse thought it was fun, because the
road was full of sticky brown mud.

But the mud stuck to his fur! More
and more mud stuck to Muddy Mouse,
until he looked like a big brown ball
of mud. The tip of his tail stuck out
of one side of the ball. The tip of his
nose stuck out of the other side.

There was so much mud on Muddy
Mouse that he couldn't walk. He
couldn't talk. He couldn't even cry,
and he wanted to cry very much.

Just then the black cat and her two
kittens came along.

They thought Muddy Mouse was a
big brown ball, so they started to play
with him. They rolled him back and
forth. They rolled him around and
around, until Muddy Mouse was dizzy.

Then the black cat and her two
kittens gave Muddy Mouse a push.
Away he rolled over the pasture. He
didn't stop until he reached the fence.

After the black cat and her two
kittens had scampered away, Father
Mouse and Mother Mouse came out
to look for Muddy Mouse. They
looked under every stone and behind
every bush.

But they would never have found
Muddy Mouse at all if he hadn't
wiggled the tip of his tail to call for
help.

Then Father Mouse and Mother
Mouse scraped and scraped and
scrubbed and scrubbed at the big
brown ball of mud.

At last they saw an ear, then a
bright little eye, then a smooth gray
back.

And after a long, long time there stood Muddy Mouse—all of him. He danced and squeaked with happiness, because he didn't have a single bit of mud on him.

Every day after that, the Mouse family still went for a walk.

And when they came to a mud puddle, Father Mouse still walked around it. Mother Mouse walked around it. Sister Mouse and Brother Mouse walked around the puddle, too.

But Muddy Mouse didn't walk around it. He *ran* around it.

Bird Talk

"Think . . ." said the robin,
"Think . . ." said the jay,
sitting in the garden,
talking one day.

"Think about people—
the way they grow:
they don't have feathers
at all, you know.

"They don't eat beetles,
they don't grow wings,
they don't like sitting
on wires and things."

"Think!" said the robin.
"Think!" said the jay.
"Aren't people funny
to be that way?"

Aileen Fisher

One Cold Day

Elizabeth Coatsworth

One cold day in late fall, a little boy got lost in the woods. The first snow had just started to fall.

He hunted east, he hunted west, but he couldn't find his way out. He hunted north, he hunted south, but he couldn't find a little house with a stove in it.

He looked up and he looked down, but he saw only trees, branches, and fallen leaves.

So he was very happy when he saw someone in a big coat coming through the woods.

The someone turned out to be an old bear in a fur cap and a muffler and mittens.

"Hello," said the old bear. "Lost, eh? Come along with me."

So the little boy went along with the bear. Pretty soon they came to a cave in the rocks. There was a small green door.

The bear opened the door with a key and turned on the lights. Inside, the cave was very cozy. There were two chairs and a table and a big old stove. The fire in the stove crackled merrily. A pot of chocolate stood at the back of the stove. There were cinnamon buns in the oven.

The old bear and the little boy had a very happy hour.

In fact, the bear asked the little boy if he didn't want to spend the winter with him.

"Of course I snooze a lot in the winter," the bear said. "I'll snooze in that chair, and you snooze in this one. We'll have a nice time."

But the little boy wanted to go home and see his family.

So the bear wrapped up again in his
big coat, his fur hat, his muffler, and
his mittens. This time he put on his
overshoes. He took the boy to the
edge of the woods and pointed his
own house out to him. The windows
in the house had just been lighted.

"Oh, thank you," said the little boy,
turning to wave. "Good night."

"He means good winter, I guess,"
said the bear to himself as he walked
back into the woods. "Anyway, I mean
to sleep all winter!" And he gave
a big yawn, and then another.

The Fox and His Bag

Old Tale

One morning a sly fox started out to market with a big empty sack over his shoulder.

On the way he caught a little bee. He put the bee into the sack and went on until he came to a house.

There he stopped and rapped on the door, rap, rap, rap!

A woman came and opened the door.

The fox said to her, "I am on my way to market. May I leave my bag here while I am gone?"

"Yes, you may," said the woman.

So the fox handed the bag to her.

"Do not open the bag while I am gone," said the fox.

Then he went on his way toward the market.

When the fox had gone, the woman took the bag into the house.

"Something is moving in that bag," she said to herself. "I wonder what it is."

So she opened the bag a little bit. Out flew the bee. It buzzed around until the woman's rooster caught it and ate it up.

When the fox came back, he opened
the bag and found it was empty.

"Where is my little bee?" he cried.

"I just looked into the bag," the
woman said, "and the little bee flew
out. My rooster ate it up."

"Then give me the rooster," said
the fox.

"You may have it," said the woman.

So the fox put the rooster into his
bag and went on his way.

Soon the fox came to another house.

A woman came to the door.

The fox said to her, "I am on my way to market. May I leave my bag here while I am gone?"

"Yes, you may," said the woman.

"Do not open the bag while I am gone," said the fox.

Then he went on his way.

The woman took the bag into the house.

"Something is moving in that bag," she said to herself. "I wonder what it is."

When she opened it, out jumped the rooster. Off he ran through the farmyard.

The woman's little boy ran after him, but the rooster got away.

After a while the fox came back for his bag. He opened the top and found the bag was empty.

"Where is my rooster?" he cried.

The woman put her arm around her little boy. "I just looked into the bag," she said, "and the rooster jumped out. My little boy ran after it, but the rooster got away."

"Then give me the little boy," said the fox.

"You may not have him," said the woman.

But the fox put the little boy into the bag anyway. Then he put the bag over his shoulder and went on his way.

Soon the fox came to another house.
Again a woman came to the door.
The fox said to her, "I am on my
way to market. May I leave my bag
here while I am gone?"

"Yes, you may," said the woman.

"Do not open the bag while I am
gone," said the fox.

Then he went on his way again.

When the fox had gone, the little
boy began to cry, "Let me out! Please
let me out!"

The woman opened the bag, and
the little boy climbed out. Then the
woman put her big dog into the bag
in the boy's place.

After a while the fox came back for
his bag. He lifted it up and found it
was as heavy as ever. He put it over
his shoulder and went off into the
woods.

"What a fine dinner I shall have!"
he said to himself.

When he reached his cave in the
woods, he opened the bag. Out
jumped the big dog. Away ran the
fox, with the dog at his heels. So the
fox did not have his fine dinner
after all.

Angus and the Ducks

Marjorie Flack

Once there was a very young little dog whose name was Angus.

Although the rest of Angus was quite small, his head was very large, and so were his feet.

Angus was curious about many places and many things.

He was curious about *what* lived under the sofa and in dark corners. And *who* was the little dog in the mirror.

From the book ANGUS AND THE DUCKS by Marjorie Flack.
Copyright 1930 by Doubleday & Company, Inc. Reprinted by permission.

He was curious about
Things-Which-Come-Apart and those
Things-Which-Don't-Come-Apart,
such as slippers and gentlemen's
suspenders and things like that.

Angus was also curious about
Things-Outdoors. But he could not
find out much about them
because of a leash.

The leash was fastened at one end
to the collar around his neck and at
the other end to Somebody Else.

But Angus was most curious of all about a noise which came from the other side of the large green hedge.

The noise usually sounded like this: "Quack! Quack! Quackety! Quack!"

But sometimes it sounded like this: "Quackety! Quackety! Quackety! Quack!"

One day the door between Outdoors and Indoors was left open by mistake. And out went Angus without the leash or Somebody Else.

Down the path he ran, until he came to the large green hedge.

He tried to go around it, but it was much too long. He tried to go over it, but it was much too high. So Angus went under the large green hedge and came out on the other side.

There, directly in front of him, were two white ducks. They were marching forward, one-foot-up and one-foot-down. "Quack! Quack! Quackety! Quack!"

Angus said, *"Woo-oo-oof!"*

Away went the ducks all of a flutter. "Quackety! Quackety! Quackety! Quackety! Quackety!"

Angus followed after.

Soon the ducks stopped by a stone
watering trough under a mulberry tree.

Angus stopped, too. Each duck
dipped a yellow bill in the clear, cool
water. Angus watched. Each duck
took a long drink of the cool, clear
water. Still Angus watched. Each
duck took another long drink of cool,
clear water.

Then Angus said, *"Woo-oo-oof!"*

Away the ducks scuttled, and
Angus lapped the cool, clear water.

Birds sang in the mulberry tree.

The sun made patterns through the leaves over the grass.

The ducks talked together. "Quack! Quack! Quack!" Then: *"Hiss-s-s-s-s-s-s! Hiss-s-s-s-s-s-s!"*

The first duck nipped Angus's tail! *"Hiss-s-s-s-s-s-s! Hiss-s-s-s-s-s-s!"*

The second duck flapped its wings!

Angus scrambled under the large green hedge, scurried up the path, scampered into the house, and crawled under the sofa. For exactly three minutes by the clock, Angus was *not* curious about anything at all.

The Old Woman and Her Pig

Old Tale

An old woman was cleaning her house when she found a little crooked sixpence. "What shall I do with this little crooked sixpence?" said she. "I will go to market and buy a little pig." So she did.

As she was coming home, she came to a stile. The pig would not go over the stile.

She went a little farther, and she met a dog. So she said to the dog, "Dog, bite pig! Pig won't go over the stile, and I shan't get home tonight." But the dog would not.

The old woman went a little farther, and she met a stick. So she said, "Stick, beat dog! Dog won't bite pig. Pig won't go over the stile, and I shan't get home tonight." But the stick would not.

She went a little farther, and she met a fire. So she said, "Fire, burn stick! Stick won't beat dog. Dog won't bite pig. Pig won't go over the stile, and I shan't get home tonight." But the fire would not.

She went a little farther, and she met some water. So she said, "Water, put out fire! Fire won't burn stick. Stick won't beat dog. Dog won't bite pig. Pig won't go over the stile, and I shan't get home tonight." But the water would not.

She went a little farther, and she met an ox. So she said, "Ox, drink water! Water won't put out fire. Fire won't burn stick. Stick won't beat dog. Dog won't bite pig. Pig won't go over the stile, and I shan't get home tonight." But the ox would not.

She went a little farther, and she met a butcher. So she said, "Butcher, kill ox! Ox won't drink water. Water won't put out fire. Fire won't burn stick. Stick won't beat dog. Dog won't bite pig. Pig won't go over the stile, and I shan't get home tonight." But the butcher would not.

The old woman went a little farther, and she met a rope. So she said, "Rope, hang butcher! Butcher won't kill ox. Ox won't drink water. Water won't put out fire. Fire won't burn stick. Stick won't beat dog. Dog won't bite pig. Pig won't go over the stile, and I shan't get home tonight." But the rope would not.

She went a little farther, and she met a rat. So she said, "Rat, chew rope. Rope won't hang butcher. Butcher won't kill ox. Ox won't drink water. Water won't put out fire. Fire won't burn stick. Stick won't beat dog. Dog won't bite pig. Pig won't go over the stile, and I shan't get home tonight." But the rat would not.

She went a little farther, and she
met a cat. So she said, "Cat, kill rat.
Rat won't chew rope. Rope won't
hang butcher. Butcher won't kill ox.
Ox won't drink water. Water won't
put out fire. Fire won't burn stick.
Stick won't beat dog. Dog won't bite
pig. Pig won't go over the stile, and
I shan't get home tonight."

Then the cat said to her, "If you
will go to yonder cow and get me
a saucer of milk, I will kill the rat."

So away went the old woman to the
cow.

But the cow said to her, "Go to
yonder haystack and get me some hay.
Then I will give you the milk."

So away went the woman to the
haystack. She brought the hay to the
cow.

As soon as the cow had eaten the
hay, she gave the old woman the milk.
Away went the old woman with a
saucer of milk for the cat.

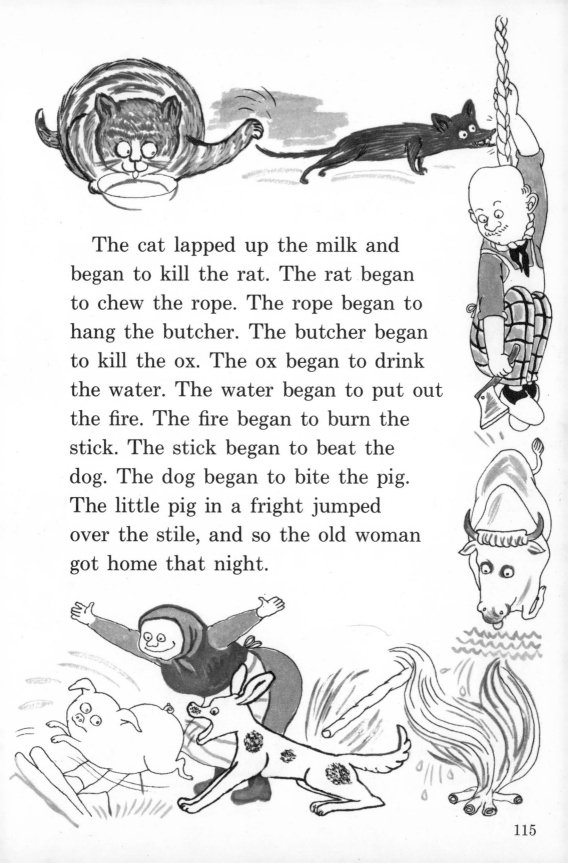

The cat lapped up the milk and began to kill the rat. The rat began to chew the rope. The rope began to hang the butcher. The butcher began to kill the ox. The ox began to drink the water. The water began to put out the fire. The fire began to burn the stick. The stick began to beat the dog. The dog began to bite the pig. The little pig in a fright jumped over the stile, and so the old woman got home that night.

Homes

A dog lives in a kennel;
　A pig lives in a pen;
A horse lives in a stable;
　And a lion, in a den.

A chicken lives inside a coop;
　And goldfish, in a bowl;
And sheep are happy in a fold;
　A mole, inside a hole.

The turtle lives inside his shell;
　The thrush lives in a nest;
But living in a little house—
　That seems to me the best.

Ilo Orleans

Wits and Wishes

If your wits are sharp,
    And you know what to do,
You can make your wishes
    All come true!

—*Barbara Shook Hazen*

Peter and the Pigeons

Charlotte Zolotow

Peter loved pigeons.

He loved the soft, slow cooooo-oooo
sound they made.

He loved the silver-gray color
of their feathers.

He loved the way they sat on
statues and hid in the carved arches
of church doors.

He loved to see them sitting like
a row of round, dark plums in the
branches of the trees.

He loved to see them flying high
and wild, in great, sweeping circles.
He loved to see them fluttering
back to earth again.

They were his friends.

"If you love pigeons so much," his
father said, "we must go to the zoo.
You will like the animals there. They
are strange animals you have never
seen before."

So Peter's father took Peter
to the zoo.

"See which animal you like best,"
his father said.

Peter looked at the lion. He was big
and kingly. Peter watched him pacing
up and down in his cage.

"I don't like him," said Peter.

Peter looked at the brown camel.
He looked at his great bony humps
and his hunched way of walking
forward.

"Not him," Peter said.

Peter looked at the red fox, with his
pointed ears and quick, catlike walk.

"Him?" said Peter's father.

"No," said Peter, "not him. Not the
fox."

Peter looked at the zebras. They
were like little, striped, white ponies.
There was a baby zebra who looked
back at Peter. Peter looked at him
for a long time.

"Him, I bet," said Peter's father.
But Peter said, "No, not him."
Peter looked at the big white
polar bears. Two lay on a rock by
a caged-in waterfall and looked like
big white rugs.

"Not you," said Peter to the bears.

Peter looked at the seals. They had small, whiskered, pointy faces, and their black coats shone in the sunlight.

"Them?" asked Peter's father.

"No," said Peter, "not them."

Peter looked at the huge, wrinkled hippopotamus. It had small, black, ugly eyes.

"Not him," said Peter. "I don't like him."

Peter looked at a great gray elephant with a long trunk and gentle eyes.

"Nor him," said Peter, "but he's nice."

Now they had seen everything in the zoo.

Peter and his father had started home when Peter suddenly said, *"Him! I like him the best."*

Peter's father stopped. He looked where Peter was looking.

A small, silver-gray pigeon was crossing the path.

Then Peter's father began to laugh.

"Of course," he said at last. "I should have known."

The Wish

Each birthday wish
I've ever made
Really does come true.
Each year I wish
I'll grow some more
And every year
    I do!

          Ann Friday

Everybody Says

Everybody says
I look just like my mother.
Everybody says
I'm the image of Aunt Bee.
Everybody says
My nose is like my father's,
But I want to look like *me*.

          Dorothy Aldis

Rain Drop Splash

Drip drop *splash!*
Drip drop *splash!*
  Went the rain all day.
Dripped
  from the shiny leaves,
Dropped
  from a rabbit's nose,
Splashed
  from a brown bear's tail.
Fell from a daisy's face,
Trickled down the tree trunks,
And *splunked*
  on a green frog's back!

Alvin Tresselt

125

Fifteen Bathtubs

Margaret Wise Brown

Once there was a little boy who lived in a house with fifteen bathtubs in it. You might think that this little boy was the cleanest little boy in the world, with fifteen bathtubs. But he wasn't.

He was the dirtiest little boy in the world. He hated to wash and he never used even one of the fifteen bathtubs.

Of course, he did take a bath once a month. But when he did take a bath, he used the garden hose. This dirty boy would run right through the water from the hose. That was the only way he took a bath, except when he took a sun bath.

He never got into one of the fifteen bathtubs.

From the book ANOTHER HERE AND NOW STORYBOOK by Lucy Sprague Mitchell. Copyright 1937 by E. P. Dutton & Co., Inc. Reprinted by permission of the publishers.

One morning the little boy got up from the breakfast table, where he had been eating jam on toast. He wiped the jam across his face with the back of his hand. Then he went out into the garden.

Now this was a clean, shining morning. All the animals were out in the warm sun.

The rabbits hopped about, and the squirrels hopped about. The butterflies flew, and the bees went buzzing all around.

So the little boy lay down to take a sun bath. He turned his jam-sticky face up to the sky and closed his eyes.

The bees buzzed in the flowers.
They flew through the air looking for
something sweet to make into honey.
Then they found the little boy's
jam-sticky face.

The little boy was asleep.
Bzzzzzzzz. A sticky treasure!

Suddenly many bees were
flying all around the little boy's face.
Zoom. Szzzz. They buzzed about his
nose and lips. Bzzzzz. They buzzed
nearer to his cheek. Szzzzz. Buzzz.
They were after the sticky, sweet jam
on his face.

The little boy jumped awake and he jumped to his feet and he jumped away. But the bees came buzzing all around right after him, trying to get the jam.

He ran and he ran, but still the bees came buzzing after him.

He ran all around the garden, and the bees buzzed all around the garden after him.

He ran and he ran into a field, and the bees buzzed through the field after him.

He ran and he ran and he ran through a wood, and the bees came buzzing after him.

Then he ran and he ran down the black tar road. The bees buzzed down the black tar road after him.

He ran and he ran up the gray gravel driveway. The bees came buzzing up the gray gravel driveway after him.

When he got to his house, he ran in the open front door. The bees came buzzing in the open front door after him.

He ran up the stairs, and the bees came buzzing up the stairs after him.

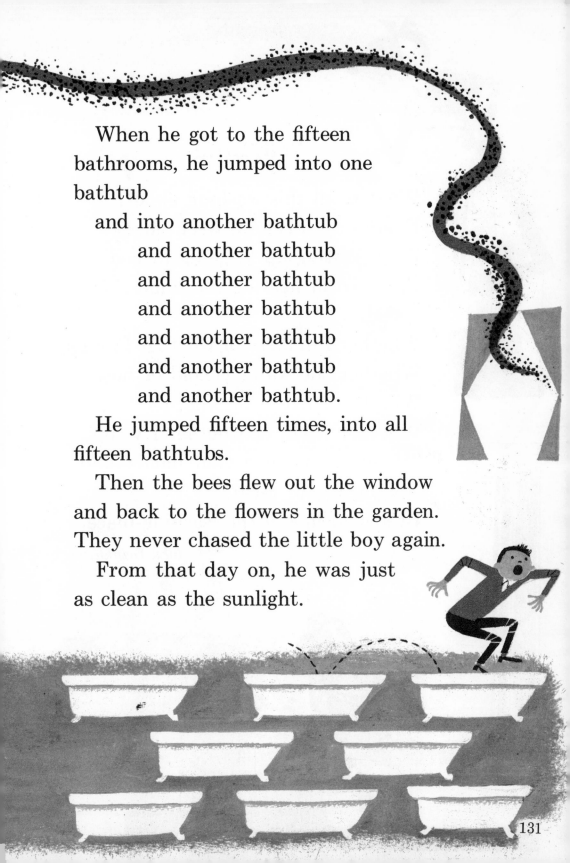

When he got to the fifteen
bathrooms, he jumped into one
bathtub
and into another bathtub
and another bathtub
and another bathtub
and another bathtub
and another bathtub
and another bathtub
and another bathtub.
He jumped fifteen times, into all
fifteen bathtubs.
Then the bees flew out the window
and back to the flowers in the garden.
They never chased the little boy again.
From that day on, he was just
as clean as the sunlight.

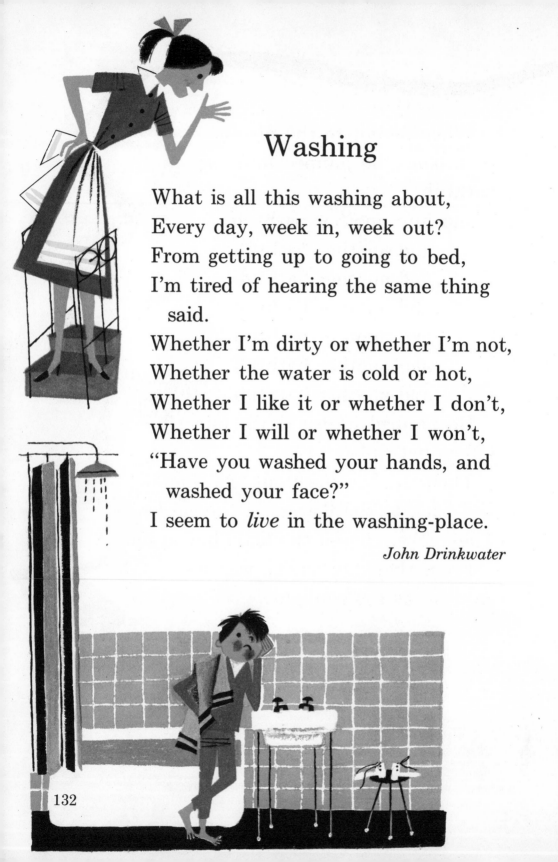

Washing

What is all this washing about,
Every day, week in, week out?
From getting up to going to bed,
I'm tired of hearing the same thing
   said.
Whether I'm dirty or whether I'm not,
Whether the water is cold or hot,
Whether I like it or whether I don't,
Whether I will or whether I won't,
"Have you washed your hands, and
   washed your face?"
I seem to *live* in the washing-place.

John Drinkwater

Jump or Jiggle

Frogs jump.
Caterpillars hump.

Worms wiggle.
Bugs jiggle.

Rabbits hop.
Horses clop.

Snakes slide.
Sea gulls glide.

Puppies bounce.
Kittens pounce.

Lions stalk—
But
I walk!

Evelyn Beyer

From ANOTHER HERE AND NOW STORYBOOK by Lucy Sprague Mitchell.
Copyright 1937 by E. P. Dutton & Co., Inc. Reprinted by permission of the publishers.

Daisy the Dinosaur

Marion Conger

On his way home from school one day, John met a dinosaur. The dinosaur was eating daisies by the side of the road.

She wagged her tail, so John held out a piece of candy. The dinosaur ate right out of his hand.

"Come home with me," said John. "I'll give you some more candy." So the dinosaur followed John home.

John's mother was in the kitchen. "Hello, dear," she said. "What happened in school today?"

"Oh, nothing," John said. "But on the way home I found a dinosaur. I'd like to keep her for a pet."

"First you wanted a collie," said his mother. "Then a great Dane. Now a dinosaur. What next?"

John could see his mother thought he was joking. But just then the dinosaur put her head through the open window.

"I promised her some candy," John said.

John's mother was too surprised to say anything. But she took a piece of candy from the shelf and held it out. The dinosaur ate it all up.

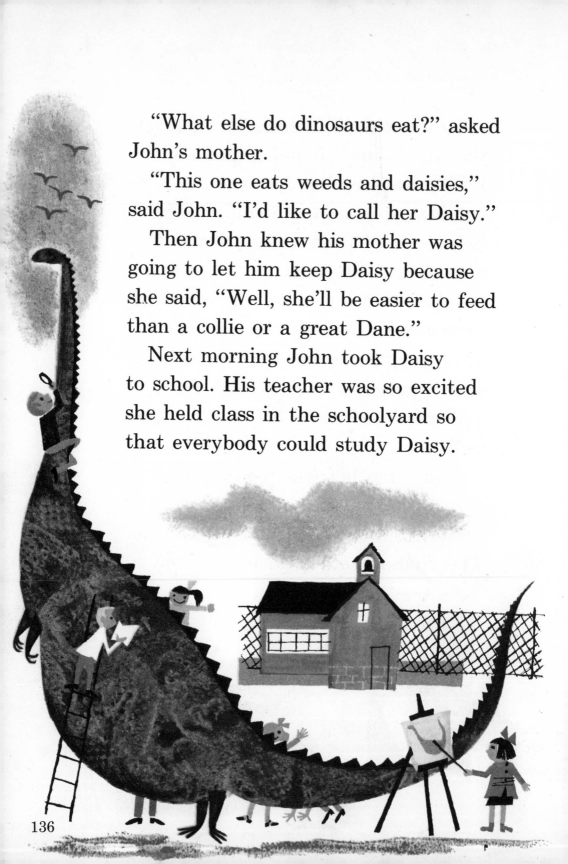

"What else do dinosaurs eat?" asked John's mother.

"This one eats weeds and daisies," said John. "I'd like to call her Daisy."

Then John knew his mother was going to let him keep Daisy because she said, "Well, she'll be easier to feed than a collie or a great Dane."

Next morning John took Daisy to school. His teacher was so excited she held class in the schoolyard so that everybody could study Daisy.

After that, on school days, Daisy
stayed at home. She was very good
about this for a few days.

Then one day she went for a walk.
Passing Mrs. Johnson's house,
she saw a beautiful bed of daisies.
They were Mrs. Johnson's pride and
joy, but they smelled good to Daisy.
They smelled so good she ate them
all up.

Mrs. Johnson was very angry. She
told John's mother she would call the
police if Daisy ever got loose again.

John had to scold Daisy. Even
though dinosaurs have tiny brains,
she seemed to know
what he meant.

That night John woke to hear fire
engines clanging down his street. They
passed John's house. They went on to
Mrs. Johnson's house.

John got dressed and raced down
the street. Daisy stayed in the yard.

Poor Mrs. Johnson! Flames were
pouring out of her house. And there
she was at a third-floor window calling
for help. The firemen were trying to
get their big ladder up to the third
floor. But it was stuck!

Away ran John. Back he came with
Daisy at his heels.

"Put your head in Mrs. Johnson's window, Daisy," he said. "Then she can slide down your back."

So Daisy put her head in the upstairs window, and Mrs. Johnson slid down. Whoosh! She slid down to the ground. She gave Daisy a great big hug, and everybody cheered.

Now Daisy goes to all the fires,
right behind the Chief's car. "It's good
to have her along," he says.

Mrs. Johnson planted a lot of new
daisies, and every day she brings Daisy
a bunch. "After all," says
Mrs. Johnson, "she saved my life."

Daisy always stays in the yard now,
except when there's a fire. And every
night she puts her head in John's
window so he can pat her good night.
She is very happy, and John is very
very proud of her.

The Young Deer, the Young Tiger, and the Fox

An Old Chinese Tale
Retold by Barbara Shook Hazen

A young deer was eating grass in
a forest high above the Yellow River.

It was summer. Everything was dry.
Both the grass and the coat of the
deer were dull yellow. It was hard to
see the deer when he moved.

But a young tiger saw the deer. He
hid behind a rock and watched him.

The young tiger had never before
left the cave where he was born.

He had never seen a deer before.
But he knew without being told that
here was something good to eat.

The young tiger walked up to the deer. The deer was afraid. He wanted to run away. Then he thought, "I would be smarter to stay where I am."

"Of what use," asked the young tiger, "are the horns on your head?"

"Oh," said the young deer, "I use them to spear tigers for my dinner."

The young tiger shook with fear.

Then he asked, "Of what use are
the white spots on your body?"

"Oh," said the young deer, "they
show how many tigers I have eaten.
Every time I kill a tiger, a white spot
appears. Shall I show you all the white
spots on my other side?"

When the young tiger heard this,
he ran away. He ran so fast that his
orange fur looked like fire.

A fox saw the young tiger running. He called, "Where are you going in such a hurry?"

The young tiger stopped running. He told the fox what the deer had said.

"You are a silly young tiger," said the fox. "The deer was only trying to trick you. Do not be afraid of him. Go back again!"

"I will not go back!" said the young tiger. "The deer will drive his horns into me. He will kill me. I know he will!"

"Then I will go back with you," said the fox. "You must let me ride on your back."

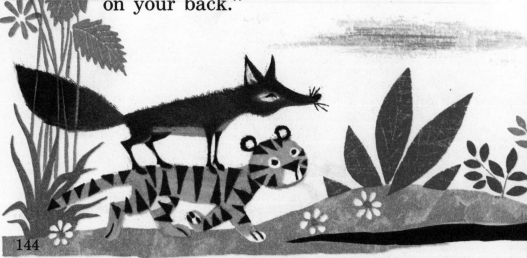

So the young tiger let the fox ride
on his back. He carried the fox back
into the forest above the Yellow River.

When he saw the fox and the young
tiger, the young deer was even more
afraid.

He wanted to run away. Then he
thought, "I would be smarter to stay
where I am."

The young deer called out in a loud
voice, "Big Brother Fox, you promised
me a tiger. The one you brought today
looks good to eat, even if it is just
a young tiger. I see you keep your
promise, and I thank you."

When the young tiger heard this, he was sure the fox had tricked him.

He ran to the cliff. He shook the fox from his back right—splash!—into the Yellow River.

Then he ran all the way back to his cave.

The young deer was safe. He held his head high. His horns were sharp, but his wits were even sharper.

Seventeen Nephews

Kathryn and Byron Jackson

Once there was a big sailor with a
merry twinkle in his bright blue eyes.

"I have seventeen nephews," he told
everyone. "I have seventeen
nephews, and every single one will be
a sailor when he's grown!"

In every port he went to, he walked
up and down the streets. Clump-clump,
went his great sea boots.
He looked in the windows of the shops.
If he saw a parrot or a monkey
or a queer clock or a puzzle,
in he went.

"I'll take seventeen of those," he said to the shopkeeper, pointing with his finger. "Yes, sir, seventeen, for my seventeen nephews who'll be sailors when they're grown."

Seventeen of this . . .

Seventeen of that . . .

Seventeen surprises from every port!
What a fine lot of surprises
that sailor had, to take home
to his seventeen nephews!

But he did have a niece. She was a very small niece, with pigtails and freckles. She could never be a sailor when she grew up.

"I know I can't be a sailor," she said, "but my uncle is a sailor. He's a very big sailor, and he may bring me a pug dog when he comes home from sea."

Her uncle never did. He just brought—

Seventeen of this . . .

Seventeen of that . . .

Seventeen of everything for his seventeen nephews who were sure to be sailors.

When he had given out the
presents, the big, merry sailor always
got seventeen thank-you's.

Then he would see his one small
niece standing in the corner.

"Who are you?" he always asked.

The very small niece said, "I'm the
one niece. I think you always forget,
Uncle, you have one niece."

"Oh, no," said the sailor. But he
always looked sad, because he *had*
forgotten. He would reach in his pocket
and find a strange coin. He always
gave the strange coin to his one
small niece and said, "There, that's
for you!"

The very small niece kept all the coins. She had a whole bag full. But they weren't parrots or monkeys or puzzles or clocks.

And they surely weren't a small pug dog.

"Next time," the niece thought. "Next time, maybe." But next time, no.

Seventeen of this . . .

And next time, no.

Seventeen of that . . . for the seventeen nephews. For the niece, the big, merry sailor had only a coin and a pat.

One day the very small niece cleaned all the coins. She put them in the bag and waited for her uncle.

In he came with his seventeen of this and his seventeen of that. And nothing for the niece except—

"Who are you?" And another strange coin . . .

But the niece said, "No, thank you, Uncle. I have lots of coins . . . Will you take them with you? And when you get to China will you spend them for a pug dog I want very much?"

"I will," her uncle promised, "and this time I *won't* forget."

Then away went her uncle,
with a merry twinkle in his eyes.

"I have seventeen nephews," he told
everybody. "They'll all be sailors. And
I have one small niece. She has
pigtails and freckles, and she's
the apple of my eye."

And the minute his ship made any
port, he went straight to the shops
and got—

Eighteen of this . . .

Eighteen of that . . .

Eighteen presents from every port.
But just *one* from China . . .

And the one present from China
was a small pug dog for one small niece
with pigtails and freckles—who could
never be a sailor when she grew up.

I Saw a Ship A-Sailing

I saw a ship a-sailing,
A-sailing on the sea;
And, oh, it was all laden
With pretty things for thee.

The four-and-twenty sailors
That stood between the decks,
Were four-and-twenty black mice
With chains about their necks.

The captain was a duck, a duck,
With a jacket on his back;
And when the ship began to move,
The captain said, "Quack, quack."

Mother Goose

154

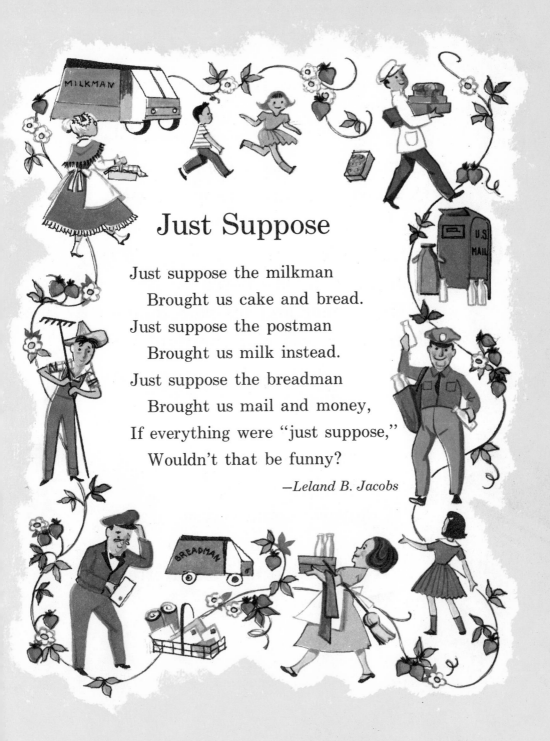

Just Suppose

Just suppose the milkman
　　Brought us cake and bread.
Just suppose the postman
　　Brought us milk instead.
Just suppose the breadman
　　Brought us mail and money,
If everything were "just suppose,"
　　Wouldn't that be funny?

　　　　　　　　—*Leland B. Jacobs*

A Cow in the House

Mabel Watts

Once there was a poor farmer.
He lived with his wife in a little
red house.

The little house had only two tiny
rooms, and a tiny porch on the side.

The farmer and his wife thought
their house was just the right size.
Then one morning the farmer's wife
made noodles.

The noodles were extra long, and
the kitchen was extra short. And there
the trouble began.

"If only we could buy a larger
house," said the farmer's wife.

And she fussed and she fretted
the whole morning long.

"We have no money to buy a larger house," said the farmer. So away he went to tell his trouble to Grandpa Wiseman.

"If you will do just as I tell you," said Grandpa Wiseman, "then everything will turn out all right."

"Indeed I will," said the farmer.

"First," said the old man, "you must take your hen into the house."

So the farmer went home, and he took his hen into the house.

The hen had never been in a house before. She did not know how to behave. She jumped up on the table and onto the farmer's lap.

At last the farmer could stand it no longer. He went to see Grandpa Wiseman.

Grandpa Wiseman said, "Now you must take the goat into the house."

So the farmer went home and took his goat into the house.

The goat ate the curtains. She slept on the bed. She smashed the chairs. She fought with the hen.

So back went the farmer to tell Grandpa Wiseman about it.

"Both the hen and the goat need company," said the old man. "Now you must go home and take your pig into the house."

"Oh, no," said the farmer, "not the pig!"

"Yes," said Grandpa Wiseman, "the pig!"

The pig took up a lot of room. He was more trouble than both the goat and the hen.

Everywhere the farmer's wife tried to put something, there was the pig.

Besides, the hen and the goat and the pig did not get along well together. Back went the farmer to tell Grandpa Wiseman about it.

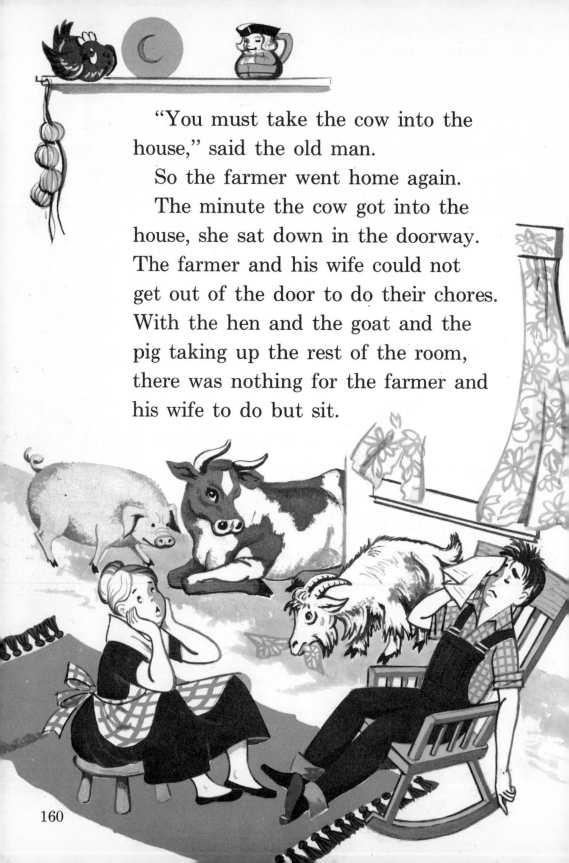

"You must take the cow into the house," said the old man.

So the farmer went home again.

The minute the cow got into the house, she sat down in the doorway. The farmer and his wife could not get out of the door to do their chores. With the hen and the goat and the pig taking up the rest of the room, there was nothing for the farmer and his wife to do but sit.

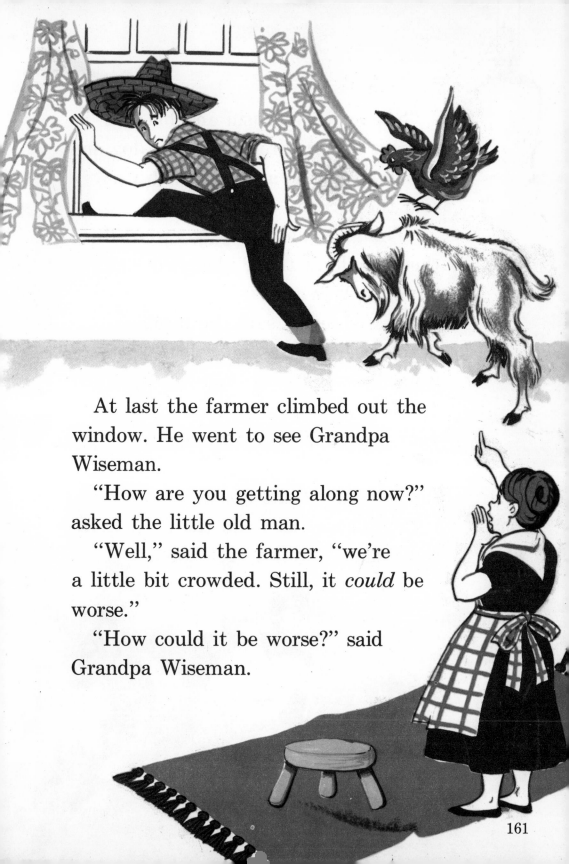

At last the farmer climbed out the window. He went to see Grandpa Wiseman.

"How are you getting along now?" asked the little old man.

"Well," said the farmer, "we're a little bit crowded. Still, it *could* be worse."

"How could it be worse?" said Grandpa Wiseman.

"Suppose my cousin and his wife and his ten children and their dog and cat should come and stay with us," said the farmer.

"Things would really be crowded then, wouldn't they?" laughed Grandpa Wiseman.

"Yes, indeed," said the farmer, "things can always get a little bit worse."

"Now we're getting somewhere with your problem," said Grandpa Wiseman. "Run home now, and push the cow out of the house."

"By all means!" said the farmer. He could hardly wait to get home.

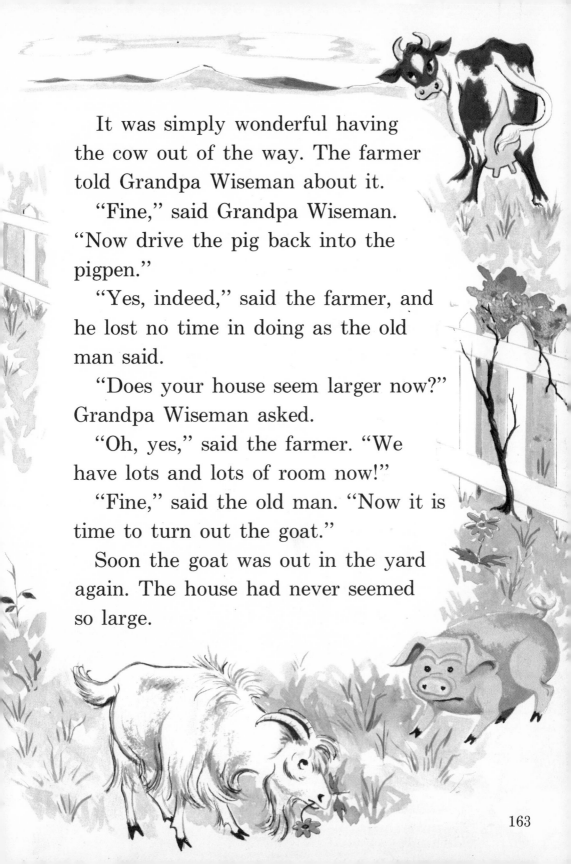

It was simply wonderful having the cow out of the way. The farmer told Grandpa Wiseman about it.

"Fine," said Grandpa Wiseman. "Now drive the pig back into the pigpen."

"Yes, indeed," said the farmer, and he lost no time in doing as the old man said.

"Does your house seem larger now?" Grandpa Wiseman asked.

"Oh, yes," said the farmer. "We have lots and lots of room now!"

"Fine," said the old man. "Now it is time to turn out the goat."

Soon the goat was out in the yard again. The house had never seemed so large.

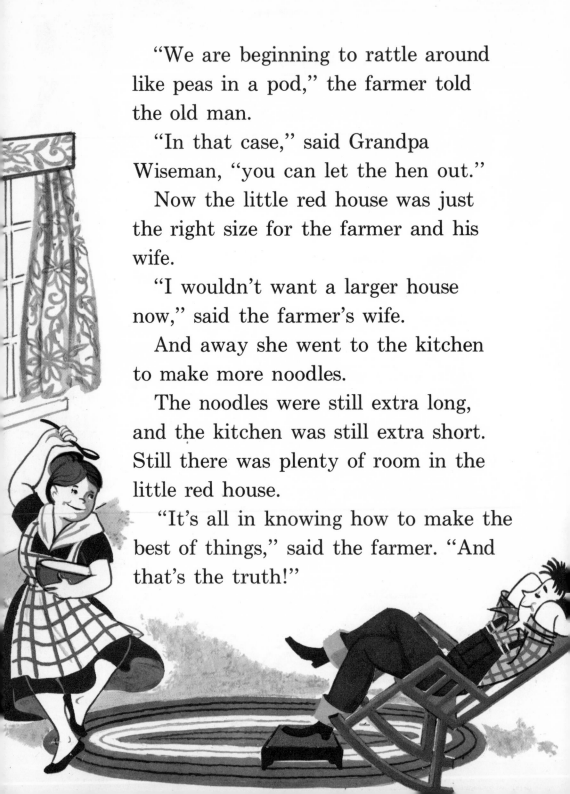

"We are beginning to rattle around like peas in a pod," the farmer told the old man.

"In that case," said Grandpa Wiseman, "you can let the hen out."

Now the little red house was just the right size for the farmer and his wife.

"I wouldn't want a larger house now," said the farmer's wife.

And away she went to the kitchen to make more noodles.

The noodles were still extra long, and the kitchen was still extra short. Still there was plenty of room in the little red house.

"It's all in knowing how to make the best of things," said the farmer. "And that's the truth!"

Grandfather Frog

Fat green frog sits by the pond,
Big frog, bullfrog, grandfather frog.
Croak—croak—croak.
Shuts his eye, opens his eye,
Rolls his eye, winks his eye,
Waiting for
A little fat fly.
Croak—croak.

I go walking down by the pond,
I want to see the big green frog,
I want to stare right into his eye,
Rolling, winking, funny old eye.
But, oh! he hears me coming by.
Croak—croak—
Splash!

Louise Seaman Bechtel

From the book ANOTHER HERE AND NOW STORYBOOK by Lucy Sprague Mitchell. Copyright 1937 by E. P. Dutton & Co., Inc. Reprinted by permission of the publishers.

Riddles

I have a little sister—they call her
    Peep-Peep;
She wades the waters deep, deep, deep;
She climbs the mountains high, high,
    high;
Poor little creature, she has but one
    eye.

                            (A star.)

                     Mother Goose

Two legs sat upon three legs
    With one leg in his lap.
In comes four legs,
    Runs away with one leg.
Up jumps two legs,
    Picks up three legs,
Throws it after four legs,
    And makes him bring back one leg.

(One leg is a leg of lamb;
two legs, a man; three legs,
a stool; four legs, a dog.)

                     Mother Goose

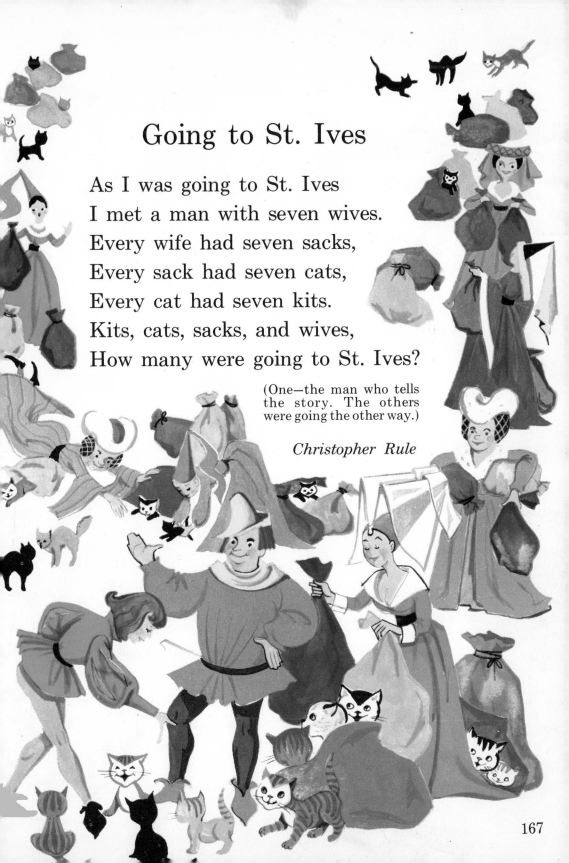

Going to St. Ives

As I was going to St. Ives
I met a man with seven wives.
Every wife had seven sacks,
Every sack had seven cats,
Every cat had seven kits.
Kits, cats, sacks, and wives,
How many were going to St. Ives?

(One—the man who tells
the story. The others
were going the other way.)

Christopher Rule

The White Goose

Tasha Tudor

The white goose was lost.

She had slipped away in the moonlight between the night and the dawn.

Robin missed her when he went to call the cows. The cows had not been waiting at the gate as usual.

The grass was silvery with frost and moonshine. Over the hill Robin could hear the cowbells. He could hear his own echo calling from the mist.

Copyright 1943 by Oxford University Press, Inc.
Reprinted by permission of Henry Z. Walck, Inc.

Robin could hear the calling of wild geese from the river. He stood still and listened. He had the feeling that something fell beside him.

He looked, and there on the grass lay a white feather. Beyond lay another white feather, and another.

Robin forgot about calling the cows. He forgot about the warm fire at home. He forgot about his mother cooking breakfast. All he saw were those white feathers lying in the moonlight. All he heard was the calling of wild geese from the river.

Robin turned off the cow path.
Down across the pasture, through
the woods, down to the marsh, he ran.

There he stopped. Beyond lay the
river.

The honking of geese was deafening.
Then, all was still. Robin looked
through the tall grasses.

There they were, the wild geese.

Among them stood a little girl,
stroking their sleek necks. She looked
up and laughed at Robin.

Robin felt the cold moonlight run through him as he listened to the girl's fairy laughter. He felt the dark eyes of the wild geese watching him.

The little girl walked toward him. "Come," said she, and took his hand.

Again Robin felt the cold touch of moonlight, and shivered.

"Come quickly," said the little girl. "It will soon be daylight. Here is a fine gander. Jump on his back and fly away with us."

"Fly away with us!" echoed the geese.

Robin hesitated. "I am thinking of home," said he.

"I know," said the little girl, "but come. We will fly over great forests and mighty rivers. All the birds of the air will talk to us."

But still Robin hesitated. "I can see my little sister smiling in her cradle," said he.

"I know," said the little girl, "but come. We will fly up that beam of moonlight to the most wonderful place you ever heard of. We will fly to the hidden side of the moon."

"The hidden side of the moon,"
echoed the geese.

"I can hear my mother singing
in the kitchen. I cannot come," said
Robin.

Then Robin saw tears running down
the little girl's face. She turned sadly
away and faded into the mist.

In her place stood the little white
goose.

173

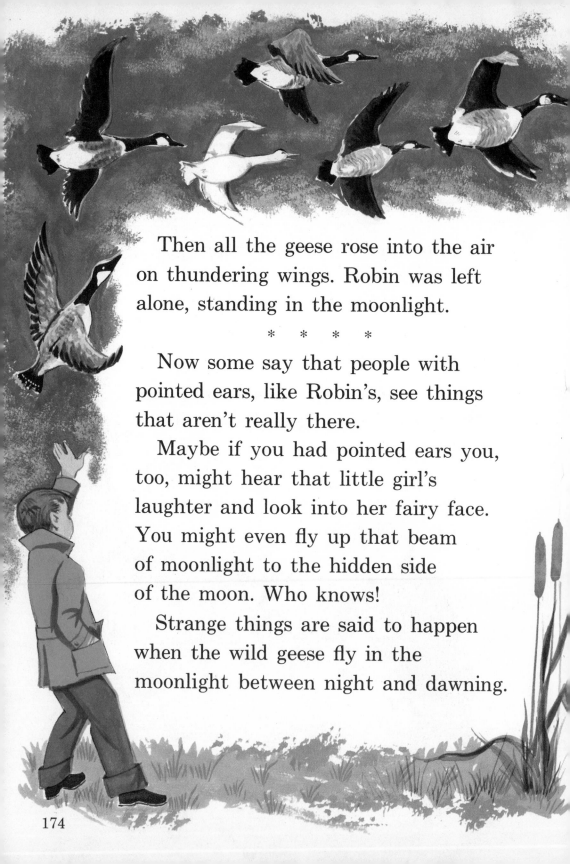

Then all the geese rose into the air
on thundering wings. Robin was left
alone, standing in the moonlight.

*   *   *   *

Now some say that people with
pointed ears, like Robin's, see things
that aren't really there.

Maybe if you had pointed ears you,
too, might hear that little girl's
laughter and look into her fairy face.
You might even fly up that beam
of moonlight to the hidden side
of the moon. Who knows!

Strange things are said to happen
when the wild geese fly in the
moonlight between night and dawning.

The Old Woman and the Strawberry Tarts

Gertrude Crampton

There was an old woman who lived
in a dell. She wouldn't and she didn't
make strawberry tarts.

She made tarts of lemon, and she
made them of lime. She made them
of pumpkin, and she made them
of peach.

But she wouldn't and she didn't
make strawberry tarts.

Every morning she packed her tarts
in a basket and carried them off
to the baker's shop.

175

Every morning the baker counted
the lemon tarts and the lime tarts,
the pumpkin tarts and the peach tarts.
He wished the old woman would make
strawberry tarts for him to sell.

"Not I," said the old woman, with
a toss of her head and her skirts.

And home she went.

"It may be," said the baker to himself, "that the old woman has no strawberries. Having no strawberries is a good reason for not making strawberry tarts."

So the baker bought all the strawberries in the town and took them to the old woman.

Later in the day, the baker got on his bicycle and rode out to the dell. He had to see how the old woman was getting along with the strawberry tarts.

But she was making strawberry jam.

And she wouldn't and she didn't make strawberry tarts.

"Maybe the old woman is very fond of strawberry jam," thought the baker. "But if she had many, many strawberries, she might have enough left over to make strawberry tarts."

Early the next morning the baker bought two hundred strawberry plants.

Then he rode his bicycle out to the dell and helped the woman plant all the fine strawberry plants.

The days went by, and the weeks went by. The rains fell, and the sun shone. The flowers bloomed, and the petals fell. And the baker dreamed of strawberry tarts.

At last the strawberries began to ripen. The baker could wait no longer. He had to see how the old woman was getting along with the strawberry tarts. So he rode his bicycle out to the dell.

But when he got there, she was making strawberry shortcake.

And she didn't and she wouldn't make strawberry tarts.

"Not I," said the old woman, with a toss of her head and her skirts.

The baker started home. But he got
no farther than the edge of the dell
when a question popped into his head.
So he rode back into the dell.

"Why?" asked the baker, very firm,
very stern, very puffed-out-in-the-chest.

"Because I don't know how," said
the old woman, very meek and very
mild.

"Why didn't you tell me before?"
asked the baker.

"Because you never did ask me,"
said the old woman, not so meek and
not so mild.

So the baker got on his bicycle. He rode like the wind to town and back.

Then he took out of his hat his great grandmother's very best recipe for making strawberry tarts.

The old woman got the first batch baked in time for supper. The baker said, "They are as good as my great grandmother's best strawberry tarts. No—they are even better."

So the old woman who lived in the dell said she would bake strawberry tarts. She would bake them for the baker to sell.

And she would and she did. For she could!

Blum

Dog means dog,
And cat means cat,
And there are lots
Of words like that.

A cart's a cart,
To pull or shove,
A plate's a plate,
To eat off of.

But there are other
Words I say
When I am left
Alone to play.

Blum is one.
Blum is a word
That very few
Have ever heard.

I like to say it,
"Blum, blum, blum"—
I do it loud
Or in a hum.

All by itself,
It's nice to sing:
It does not mean
A single thing.

Dorothy Aldis

A Good Man
and His Good Wife

Ruth Krauss

Once there was a good man and he had a good wife.

They lived in a beautiful cottage. It had white walls and red curtains and lots of little cubbyholes and handy shelves.

The man and his wife were very happy, except that he could never find things.

Copyright 1944 by Harper & Brothers. Copyright 1950 by Ruth Krauss and Ad Reinhardt

He would look for his shoes and he
could not find his shoes.

He would look for a book and he
could not find the book.

He would go to feed the canary and
he could not find the birdseed.

But this made no difference, because
he could not find the canary. He could
find nothing.

Then the good man would say,
"This is ridiculous!" He would walk
up and down the room and shake his
head and say very loudly, "This is
ridiculous indeed!"

But it was not his fault. He could
not find anything because his good
wife had moved everything.

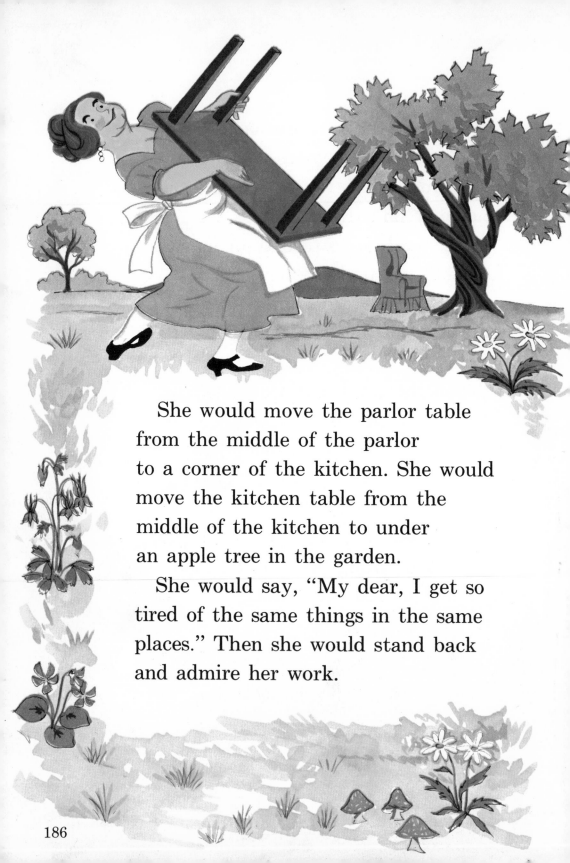

She would move the parlor table
from the middle of the parlor
to a corner of the kitchen. She would
move the kitchen table from the
middle of the kitchen to under
an apple tree in the garden.

She would say, "My dear, I get so
tired of the same things in the same
places." Then she would stand back
and admire her work.

She moved the clock from the wall
above the bed to an end of the shelf
in the parlor.

She moved her good man's Sunday
clothes from the closet in the hall
to the closet in the attic.

She moved his favorite chair from
its place before the fire to a corner
of the bedroom.

She moved everything in the little
house.

She said, "Yes, yes, I do get so tired
of the same things in the same
places!"

Then the good man had to learn
where things were all over again.

But by the time he learned to find his fishing rod in the broom closet next to the pantry, everything was changed again.

Again he looked very stern and cried, "This is ridiculous!"

He decided to do something about it. He said, "I will do something about it," and smiled to himself. He said, "I'll settle this once and for all."

And he did something about it.

He put his shoe on his head.

He wore his garters around his neck.

He tied his necktie around his knee.

He wore his trousers for his coat
and his coat for his trousers, and both
of them upside down.

He wore his spectacles on his elbow.

He wore his socks on his ears.

Then he crawled downstairs.

He sat on the breakfast table, ate
his napkin, and wiped his face
on a biscuit.

When his good wife saw him, she opened her eyes wide. She dropped the dishes. She opened her mouth wide in surprise. She threw up her hands.

Then she cried, "My dear, this is ridiculous!"

He did not reply, but went on buttering his napkin and chewing little pieces off it, and wiping his face with the biscuit. His garters jingled around his neck, and his socks flopped on his ears.

Then she cried again, "But, truly, this is ridiculous, this is just too ridiculous!"

"But, my dear," he said very quietly, "I get so tired of the same things in the same places."

So that was how the good man cured his good woman of a bad habit.

And they lived even more happily than before in their beautiful cottage with its white walls and red curtains and little cubbyholes and handy shelves. Nowadays when the good man wants to read a book, he knows that he will find it in the bookcase.

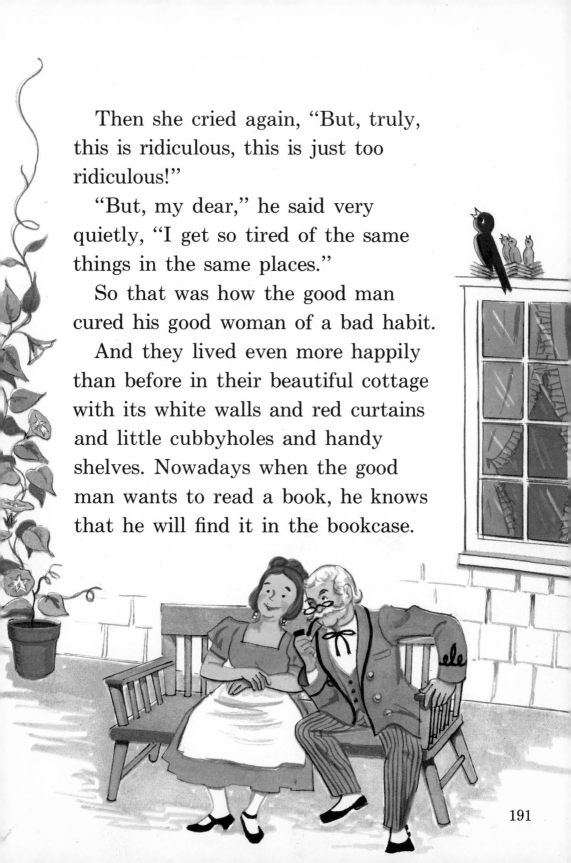

ACKNOWLEDGMENTS

The editors wish to extend their thanks and appreciation to the following authors, publishers, and periodicals for kindly granting us permission to reprint selections in this volume.

ABELARD-SCHUMAN LIMITED for BIRD TALK from *Up the Windy Hill* by Aileen Fisher. Copyright 1953 by Aileen Fisher. —CHILD LIFE for THE WISH by Ann Friday. Copyright 1955 by Child Life. —WM. COLLINS SONS & CO., LTD. for WASHING from *More About Me* by John Drinkwater. —PAT DAY for THE MOUSE'S HOUSE from *Jack and Jill.* Copyright 1956 by The Curtis Publishing Company. —FOLLETT PUBLISHING COMPANY for A COW IN THE HOUSE by Mabel Watts. Copyright 1956 by Follett Publishing Company. —GOLDEN PRESS, INC. for the following selections, copyright in the years indicated by Golden Press, Inc.: LOU STICK and THE OLD WOMAN AND THE STRAWBERRY TARTS from *The Golden Funny Book* by Gertrude Crampton (1950); SEVENTEEN NEPHEWS from *Pirates, Ships and Sailors* by Kathryn and Byron Jackson (1950); THE WILD WHITE HORSE and HOW THE CHIPMUNK GOT HIS STRIPES from the Giant Little Golden Book *Cowboys and Indians* by Willis Lindquist (1958); PRETENDING from *The Animal Fair* by Alice and Martin Provensen (1952); THE DOG AND THE ROOSTER from *Nursery Tales,* edited by Elsa Jane Werner (1952); HI! HO! THREE IN A ROW from the Little Golden Book of the same title by Louise Woodcock (1954). —HENRY HOLT AND COMPANY, INC. for THE STORY THAT NEVER ENDS from *A Rocket in My Pocket* by Carl Withers. Copyright 1948 by Henry Holt and Company, Inc. —LOTHROP, LEE AND SHEPARD CO., INC. for THE WONDERFUL FEAST by Esphyr Slobodkina. Copyright 1955 by Lothrop, Lee and Shepard Co., Inc.; and RAINDROP SPLASH from the book of the same title by Alvin Tresselt. Copyright 1946 by Lothrop, Lee and Shepard Co., Inc. —ILO ORLEANS for RIDES from *Child Life.* Copyright 1953; and HOMES from *The Instructor.* Copyright 1951. —THE MEDICI SOCIETY LTD. and G. P. PUTNAM'S SONS for EVERYBODY SAYS from *Everything and Anything* by Dorothy Aldis. Copyright 1927 by Minton, Balch & Co., renewed 1955 by Dorothy Aldis. —G. P. PUTNAM'S SONS for BLUM from *All Together* by Dorothy Aldis. Copyright 1952 by G. P. Putnam's Sons. —STORY PARADE, INC. for ONE COLD DAY by Elizabeth Coatsworth. Copyright 1952 by Story Parade, Inc. —FREDERICK WARNE & CO., INC. for SUSAN BLUE by Kate Greenaway, from *Marigold Garden.* Copyright 1910 by Frederick Warne, Inc. —THE JOHN C. WINSTON COMPANY for THE FOX AND HIS BAG from *The Winston First Reader,* Sidney G. Firman, Ethel H. Maltby. Copyright 1918, 1920, 1926, 1928 by The John C. Winston Company.